"This is a book to go he~
day-to-day life and l
sion towards children   ~ar to
the Creator."
—*Evelyn Lam Yeewah,* ~   *~ul, CCC Heep Woh College,*
Hong Kong

"I highly recommend this book to families with kids who love
learning about our Creator—God. Through the dialogues
between two adorable cats, Shakespeare and Dickens, parents
and their kids can explore the mystery …

> In the beginning there was just darkness. No lights. No fire-
> flies. No sun, moon, or stars. No people. No animals. No
> vets or rabies shots or litter boxes or cat treats or creepy
> crawlies or flea collars or…

"Think about how your kids' imaginations could stretch!"
—*Doris Chan Sau Ling, Former English Panel Chair, CCC Heep
Woh College, Hong Kong*

"This book tackles an immense topic—creation—through the
eyes of a small creature, a feline named William Shakespeare
Davis. The story is charmingly told through a Christian per-
spective in a way that makes it accessible to children, though
adults may find themselves pulled into the story as well."
—*Susan Lapin, author, wife, and business partner of Rabbi Daniel
Lapin, Seattle, WA*

In the Beginning

The Story of Creation as Witnessed by Shakespeare the Cat

M E Weldon

Mobile, Alabama

In the Beginning
by M E Weldon
Copyright ©2014 M E Weldon

ISBN 978-1-58169-545-8
For Worldwide Distribution
Printed in the U.S.A.

Evergreen Press
P.O. Box 191540 • Mobile, AL 36619
800-367-8203

*This book is dedicated
to my grandchildren,
Victoria and James,
who have shared my life's adventures
long distance while allowing me
to travel the world.
I love you.*

ACKNOWLEDGMENTS

With special thanks to:

My prayer team (I call them Team Joy)—a group of friends and family who have prayed for and supported me since before I left the U.S. in 1998.

My son, Whitney, and his wife, Daphne—the parents of my precious grandchildren. I love you and am so proud of the people you have become.

My daughter, Tobey, and her husband, Chad—my most faithful prayer support team. This will be the year of rebuilding for all of us!

Linda, my best friend in Oklahoma City; Monna, my best friend in Tulsa; Karen, my best friend in Crete; Wilma, my best friend in Abu Dhabi; Lois, my best friend in HK; Mary, my best friend in Fort Worth/Egypt; and those best friends in lands yet to be visited.

My pastors, Larry and Tiz Huch. Your insight into the Jewish roots of the Bible have inspired me and given me such great ideas for the upcoming adventures of Shakespeare and Dickens.

My agent and publisher. Thank you for your faith in me.

FOREWORD

In the Beginning is a treasure chest of a tale brought about through the real-life adventures of M E Weldon in her quest to teach children about the wonders of God and His creation through various mediums of imagination and fun.

Of all the children she's taught and loved, I am the most blessed and the greatest beneficiary as her proud and grateful daughter. And, as M E Weldon's number one fan, it is my privilege and responsibility as an eyewitness to the tale (and tails!) to herald this unprecedented and brilliantly imaginative story with highest praise and recommendation!

With vibrant scenes and explosive antics, the personalities of the two cat brothers jump off the page to become a fur-filled, action-packed movie in the reader's mind. As a powerful antidote to the secular and mystical, M E Weldon intertwines the masterful retelling of the creation story by Shakespeare the cat with the constant interruptions and faux pas of his younger brother, Dickens, who represents the curiosity in all of us.

Through Dickens, M E Weldon asks—and helps answer—the questions we all have deep inside. This is a story for the child of God in all of us.

—*Tobey Kay Bullington, #1 daughter*

~ 1 ~

Shakespeare was trying so very hard to sleep. He kept hearing clicking or tapping noises and did not want to wake up enough to explore. He kept thinking to himself that it had to be either water dripping in the sink again or that pesky bird outside tapping on the window. Although annoying, neither of those choices merited him totally waking up to investigate.

His whiskers twitched and he kept changing positions. Finally, he could stand it no longer and opened one sleepy green eye. Across the room from where he slept sat his brother, busily typing away on their mom's laptop.

Angrily—oh so angrily—Shakespeare growled through clenched teeth. "Dickens! What in the world are you doing? I am trying to sleep here."

Dickens looked hurt. "I'm working on your story, brother. Listen to what I've got so far."

Shakespeare slowly began the process of moving from a trying-to-sleep position to a now-what-has-he-done position so he could focus on his brother.

Dickens cleared his throat and began reading in his annoyingly nasal, monotone voice, "It was a dark and stormy night. One of those nights when no matter how many times Mom or Dad come into the room to look under the bed to prove there are no monsters, a child can still hear them in the closets, behind the door, in the attic, even outside the window!"

The tapping and droning continued—for Dickens was quite adept at composing and typing at the same time. The tapper was unaware that a storm was developing on the other side of the room.

"Once more, Mom or Dad would come in, turn on the lights, look round, and say, 'See, there's nothing here. It's just the wind. Now go to sleep!' And then they'd be gone, and the child left in the dark with them—the antsypantsysnigs or the crummiedummiedeediddles, or even worse, the qwertzysniggleedoodums!"

At that, the brewing storm erupted into volcanic proportions!

"Okay. That is enough, Dickens! What is the matter with you?"

Shakespeare had been sitting quietly, perched beside the computer screen, listening ever so carefully to what was being read. But now he reached his long, furry paw out and boxed his brother's ears. His brother did not take very kindly to this treatment in the least.

Shakespeare continued, "I never ever said anything about moms, dads, beds, monsters, or whatever in the world else you're talking about!"

"I'm setting the scene, Dude," Dickens replied a bit defensively. "I'm coloring the tone; I'm laying the groundwork; I'm casting the mood for your—dare I say the word—tale."

He felt, you see, that this was some of his best work. He sat massaging his stinging ears with his paws, looking quite forlorn. *Shakespeare is always trying to make me feel stupid*, he thought angrily.

Now before this brotherly spat erupts into epic proportions, let's clear the air, shall we? I think I might be able to "hear" what you, faithful reader, are thinking at this point. Shall I venture a guess?

Aha! Whoa! Wait a minute. Dickens? Shakespeare? Whiskers? Paw? Laptop?

You're confused, aren't you? Yes, well, let's see. How does one explain Shakespeare, Dickens, and a computer in the same time frame? For want of a better idea, let's just start at the beginning, shall we?

We have to start with Miss Mattie Davis, an English teacher on assignment in a faraway land. Miss Mattie was a great reader who loved collecting things—cookbooks (she was an amazing cook), crystal candle holders, teapots, and books—mysteries, classics, and history. But she confessed to some other addictions too—chocolate, watches (she had over twenty), leather wallets (she couldn't begin to remember how many she had), and lots of silver bracelets.

Miss Mattie was a tall—no make that a very tall—woman with long, curly brown hair and enormous blue eyes. She loved wearing bright colors and lots of jewelry. On her right arm, she wore bracelets she'd collected from the countries she visited.

Sometimes she'd use more than ten at a time. Sometimes one or more broke, got lost, or most probably, she gave it away—making the average total about seven that she'd wear at a time. She always jingled when she walked or wrote or typed.

Miss Mattie was also a witty lady with a lot of friends. As mentioned before, she was very, very tall—which made life in this present country a bit difficult as she was at least a foot or more taller than the general public. Her feet always hung off the beds—no matter where she was—and over the edge of her small loveseat when she stretched out to read. But since she lived alone, it was no problem most times.

When Miss Mattie moved away from her home and family and into this particular flat (for that was what apartments were called in the new country), she kept busy at her job (she was a teacher) and with her social life. But in her home, she grew lonely and began to search for a pet to keep her company. She wanted no dogs, though, since they have to be walked and their barking might disturb the neighbors. After a while, Miss Mattie heard about a tiny kitten she thought would be perfect.

One evening in an underground train station, Miss Mattie met her friend Doris who was carrying a noisy cardboard shoebox. In it was a howling little kitty that a roommate had adopted but couldn't keep because someone else in her flat was allergic to cats. It fell to Doris to get rid of the little allergen.

Even at that tender age, this kitten seemed quite indignant at the rough and shoddy treatment he felt was being meted out to him. He set up a loud protest that could be heard by most of the passersby on the busy street.

Both Doris and Miss Mattie were worried about being arrested for animal cruelty, so they decided it best for Miss Mattie to get him home as quickly as possible. The most direct and fastest way to her flat was by the underground train, so since she was right next to the station, Miss Mattie thought this to be the best option.

She ducked into the station, used her pass to get through the gate, and waited for the next train going in her direction. She had to ignore the stares of fellow train travelers who were curious about the wiggling, howling box she was carrying.

Animals are not allowed on the subway train (apart from guide dogs), but Miss Mattie really had no other way to get home in a hurry so, in the end, she was carrying a concealed kitten! She tried to look as though nothing was out of the ordinary in spite of all the howling, spitting, and hissing coming from inside the box, but my how the people stared at her!

She sat silently praying that the conductor would not come along and put her and the baby kitten off the train. Thankfully, no such misadventure occurred and in due time, Miss Mattie and her mysterious box were in the elevator of her building. (By the way, those howls of protest really sounded lion-like inside the elevator.)

Once inside her flat, Miss Mattie put the box on the floor and loosened the lid just a bit. What happened next reminded her of a jack-in-the-box toy as the top flew open and out sprang a black and white ball of very angry kitten fur! (Despite this initial transport, the kitten grew into a stately older cat who somehow still had a curious attraction to boxes. If there were a box in sight, rest assured, the cat would find a way to get into it and hide.)

In her home country, Miss Mattie had lots of cats, and they were all named for characters or authors connected to her favorite works of literature. She had a female named Guinevere and three males named Chaucer, Percy, and Emerson. From her first look at the new kitten, Miss Mattie had decided she was going to call the kitten Poirot (after the famous Belgian detective in Agatha Christie's mystery books). After all, he did have a tiny little half moustache. But the little scamp soon showed her that he had his own ideas of what his name should be.

For you see, he developed a sort of addiction to her pens. Indeed, no pen was safe from his clutches, though he didn't seem to care much for pencils. One wonders why. If Miss Mattie left a red marking pen on the table when she went to get another cup of tea, she had to conduct a full scale search for that same pen when she returned. If she found it, it was often underneath the sofa or sometimes in a completely different room.

The kitten also had a rather peculiar fondness for perching on books in his early days. Whenever he found a book left open, the kitten could not rest until he had scampered across the room, leapt up onto the table or chair, and plopped down on the book. What was it—the smell of the ink? The feel of the paper? The subject matter? No one really knew the answer. Perhaps he was simply resting. Whatever the reason, this odd little fellow seemed to have indicated his name must be something more in line with paper and pen—writing for sure. And so at last, he was named after the great author, poet, and literary master of words, William Shakespeare.

Another early quirk of Shakespeare's that he never quite outgrew was a passion for feet—and shoes. When just a tiny kitten, he would stalk Miss Mattie's feet if he ever found them propped up on the sofa or a table. Of course, when he leapt high in the air to attack, those needle-sharp claws found their way into her tender feet, which meant Shakespeare would find himself sailing through the air towards whatever piece of furniture was in the line of fire. Somehow that rude treatment never served to deter him from his next adventure with feet, however much trouble it caused him.

When Miss Mattie's students came to visit, the first thing they'd do when entering her flat was to remove their shoes. Soon after—very soon—all the visitors were surprised to find this tiny kitten (and in later years, very super-sized adult cat) sniffing around their shoes. Sometimes he would even get inside the shoes and peek out at them comically. He was definitely full of surprises and always seemed to know instinctively which people were afraid of cats, which were allergic to them, or even better, which were wearing black clothes!

Indeed, because she had acquired him for companionship, Miss Mattie had initially hoped that Shakespeare would be her sleeping companion and keep her feet toasty warm. In this particular tropical country, there was no central heat in the buildings, and the winter evenings did get quite chilly. Miss Mattie hoped a warm furry cat would be just the ticket. Well, that is what she had hoped before she discovered her new kitten's "issues."

Soon after the manifestation of his foot fetish (for that is what she began to call it), she also discovered that Shakespeare wanted to sleep under the covers. You can well imagine what happened when Miss Mattie's bare feet moved during her slumber. It only took one or two nights of surprise attacks on her feet for Miss Mattie to decide Shakespeare had to sleep elsewhere.

At first Miss Mattie developed the habit of merely shutting her bedroom door when she retired for the evening. However, that left a curious kitten loose in her flat. The resulting bangs, booms, and crashes kept her out of her bed more than in it—so that practice was quickly moved to the been-there-done-that file.

Finally, in desperation, Miss Mattie settled on the perfect plan. Based on something she had read in the Lillian Jackson Braun *Cat Who. . .* books, she lured the kitten into her tiny office with a small spoonful of tinned gourmet cat food. Then she would place the dish on the floor, say "Good night, Shakespeare"; and while he was devouring the treat, she would firmly latch the door, making quite sure beforehand that nothing breakable was within his reach. She figured she had covered all the bases and confidently assured herself that this plan was going to work.

The first night or two, there was a lot of howling, hissing, and meowing coming from the secure environment, but Miss Mattie stood firm—and soon the new bedtime habit was set.

~ 2 ~

And now it was this very Shakespeare who was directing his subdued fury at the other feline in the Davis family. Although Shakespeare, the larger cat, was missing a considerable chunk of his t-a-i-l, he had still grown into quite a handsome and intelligent fellow.

When Miss Mattie had first met him, he was so tiny and wiggly that she hadn't noticed anything missing on his anatomy. But as he grew, "it" became more noticeably short. No one ever really knew the whole story of how Shakespeare lost his, umm, you-know-what, but lose it he did. And the bit that was left was a tad crooked, which left him looking a bit wobbly and unstable on his massive legs. As a result, he was quite sensitive about its . . . umm . . . lack of presence, thank you very much. Cats take great pride in their long, luxurious you-know-whats! Thus, everyone was extremely careful not to mention its condition when Shakespeare was around.

Unexplainably, he had an uncanny knowledge about ancient history—extremely ancient history—and it was his heartfelt desire to get his version of the tales (it's not the same spelling, so it can be said) down before he forgot any of the facts. So now here he was trying to do his best to get all his experiences recorded and saved for posterity, and his brother was mucking about and causing all manner of headaches. Actually, it seemed that whenever Dickens was involved, headaches and trouble usually followed very close behind.

Indeed, Shakespeare's current predicament had its start when he was about two human years old. You see, each summer Miss Mattie went back to her own country to visit her family, and she always felt like such a bad mother when she had to leave Shakespeare alone, even though someone usually stayed in the flat while she was away. So the first year that he was part of her family, just before she left for summer holiday, she brought Shakespeare a present she thought he would really love: a teddy bear.

He adored that bear. He carried it from room to room even though it was almost the same size as he. He loved it until it was quite raggedy. It had been washed and washed and washed until it quite disintegrated and had to be thrown in the rubbish.

The next year she brought him a stuffed monster toy in a hideous shade of green that shook when touched and made horrid noises. Shakespeare would never admit to being afraid, but that green thing, he quite ignored! He wanted his teddy bear, but it was long gone.

So, the year to which we refer, Miss Mattie felt that she had at last found the right thing to keep Shakespeare company: a baby brother! When she left the flat that fateful day, she told Shakespeare that she was going to bring him a big surprise when she returned. He could hardly settle down for his nap for wondering what it was. He dreamt of fish, or big tins of his favorite night-time treat, or teddy bears! Surely it was a new teddy bear!

Sure enough, Miss Mattie was smiling and singing when she brought the large plastic box in and set it on the floor. Shakespeare had a funny feeling in his tummy because somehow, he instantly knew what it was. (Cats have great smellers, you know!)

Oh joy, thought Shakespeare at the time, *just what I need: a wormy, loud-mouthed kid with a long, pointy tail to have to share my bed, my food, and my toys with!* He hissed and huffed and showed quite an attitude. Later, he did put on a good act, pretending that he liked the baby. But he really wasn't thrilled in the least. In fact, brotherly love was the furthest thing from his mind when he peeked into that carrier and saw this orange furball looking back at him.

The new baby was already quite an expert in horrifying experiences by the time Miss Mattie had found him. He had been snatched from the rubbish bins on the streets of their busy city by a nurse who rescued homeless cats as a sort of hobby. She kept all her rescuees—about twenty-five cats at the time—in towers of cages in her small sitting room. Oh my, that room was noisy, crowded, and smelly!

Miss Mattie's friend took her to visit the nurse to see if there might be a proper companion for Shakespeare. For several months, Miss Mattie had been searching for a tiny girl kitty so Shakespeare could become a protective big brother. But instead she felt her heart drawn to a three-month-old golden orange kitten with beautiful ginger-colored eyes. He wasn't really orange and he was certainly not gold. But what was white was really, really white. And the part that was golden orange was . . . well, you know.

The kitten somehow seemed to know that this lady was trying to decide which of his fellow felines to take home, and even though he didn't know her or what her home was like, he felt it had to be better than his current accommodations. So he tried his best to explain his particular case to her. He meowed so pitifully that she couldn't look at or consider another cat. Although he was ever so timid, he purred so loudly and looked so very sad that he just simply won her heart.

Soon he was being forcibly removed from his cage

and stuffed into a blue plastic cat carrier. You see, Miss Mattie had learned her lesson about the subway train with Shakespeare, and now she had a proper carrier with her and an even more proper taxi waiting!

While being bounced and jostled around in the cage on the way home, the kitten had ample time to question his sanity at trying so hard to get out of his safe and quiet cage. Many times during the long, bumpy ride home, he asked himself, "What was I thinking?" Miss Mattie developed a habit during that long ride that continues to this very day—she would stick a few fingers inside the cage and massage the kitten's head and nose. He especially loved it when she stroked his wide nose and would be quiet for a few seconds. But soon, he began meowing so loudly and with such a booming voice, it always prompted Miss Mattie to remark, "How does something so small have such a loud mouth?"

It only grew worse when Miss Mattie arrived home and put the carrier down on the floor. At first, she left the door to the cage locked. The kitten thought "Great! Now I'm in a locked plastic cage—at least the other one was wire so I could look around." Suddenly, he was aware of a sinister presence that made the hair on his body stick out just like in that *Jaws* movie just before the shark leapt out of the water.

Shakespeare had naturally trotted over to investigate.

That, after all, is what cats who were almost named Poirot do best! He took quite a few steps in the direction of the blue box on the sitting room floor. Then he stopped and every part of his body seemed to go stiff. Soon he erupted with quite a concerto of howling, yowling, hissing, and spitting.

Inside the carrier, the younger cat was properly terrified because he understood fully that this monster was genuinely angry and quite rude in his hissing and spitting, and that he most certainly did not like what was inside, not one tiny bit! He resolved to stay in that carrier forever—no matter what!

When the door to the carrier was opened, the newcomer huddled far in the back and would not come out. Instead he waited until the coast was clear and finally ran out and hid under the bed in the guest room, where he stayed for many long hours, afraid for his very life. His reception when finally he did venture out was chilly, to say the least. For Shakespeare, confident that his stern warning to the intruder would be heeded, had turned his back and returned to the sitting room and his favorite spot and was soon sound asleep—well, as soundly as someone could sleep with one eye ready to pop open at a moment's notice.

Miss Mattie felt it best to let the boys (for this is what she always called them) work this out by themselves. So after she had assured herself that they were in no mortal danger, she left them to get acquainted and went in the sitting room to work on her schoolwork. From time to time, Shakespeare kept returning to the guest room/office door, out of sight of the terrified newcomer inside. When finally he gave up his post and went into the sitting room to stay with his mother, Shakespeare felt confident that whatever was inside the guest room would possibly stay there forever.

It was much, much later that night when the new kitten ventured to the door of the guest room, peered down the hallway toward the sitting room, and took one timid step outside. Two things happened almost at once. Shakespeare leapt out of Miss Mattie's lap, hissing all the way. And Miss Mattie stood up and shouted "Shakespeare! You leave that baby alone!" Both of these events sent the baby right back under the bed.

After a stern lecture from his mother, Shakespeare calmed down and was determined to at least try and make the best of this situation. Miss Mattie went into the guest room, got down on the floor, and tried to coax the kitten from under the bed. Right then, he began to firmly develop his fear of all things human—even his mother. In fact, it could be said that this kitten was afraid of anything moving. He was just the most skittish animal alive—his mother swore to it!

Eventually the new baby came out and got acquainted with his older brother. They had a few nose sniffing moments, which Miss Mattie watched from afar, whilst holding her breath. He soon came to be called Charles Dickens due to his humble beginnings in the rubbish bins. However, his name was soon shortened to Dickens because of his tendency to always seem to be right smack in the middle of trouble.

It took many days and weeks of hissing and spitting, but the two siblings did eventually develop a family bond and spent many happy hours napping together on their favorite sofa. And Shakespeare did have to admit that Dickens was a great comfort to him when their mother left them to go on holidays. But he did have this terribly annoying habit of always causing minor catastrophes.

~ 3 ~

Because they were locked in the guest room/office at night, it wasn't long before Dickens began to show unusual prowess at computer skills. Perhaps because of the fact that he napped on the warm keyboard while his mom was out, he developed a strong attachment to the laptop even while he slept. Whatever had happened to him in his first months on the street, he knew an awful lot about technology. If the laptop weren't latched completely, Dickens was able to get the top up and was soon doing an enormous amount of snooping in Miss Mattie's files. He did always restrain himself from making any corrections or additions, however. He just looked and never ever touched—most of the time.

As the two of them grew from being kittens, they were quite a pair. The chubby, golden-orange cat with the enormous ginger-colored eyes had a broad white and pink nose. He had a snow-white tummy and very slender white legs and feet. However, it took only one look in those ginger eyes for a person to know that this was a cat that could cause serious complications to even the most well thought out plans. And oh my goodness, how he loved his food—in fact, he loved everybody's food. It's a wonder that his older brother ever survived!

The stately and noble older brother was sleek and shiny with an equally snowy white tummy, though it sagged a bit when he walked—evidence of his sedentary lifestyle, perhaps. His back had great black spots, as if a painter had carelessly dripped great blobs of paint on him. His always alert green eyes seemed like windows into his complex cat soul. They could narrow into evil-looking slits at the drop of a hat or at the mention of something he found distasteful. But there was a look in those eyes that gave evidence that this cat was determined to discover the answer to the mysteries around him—whether the mysteries be a new bauble hanging on the front doorknob or a partially closed (therefore open) closet door.

As the cats grew, Miss Mattie soon discovered two very important things. First, inside cats could not have front claws or her furniture and draperies (as well as her legs and feet) would surely suffer. This involved a very simple operation in her home country but was very difficult to arrange in this current one.

The second thing was that male cats who are kept inside all the time do need a little surgical alteration to keep them from doing what male cats do to attract girl-friends. Shakespeare had had both alterations performed before his brother came along so the new addition to the family had only to wait his turn.

Oh, my. Let's see now. How did we get so far from that dark and stormy night? Shall we get back to Shakespeare's, um, story?

Our feline champions were at the beginning of what promised to be quite a spat. How they got to that point was by a somewhat logical path, sort of. Right from the start, once the boys got over their initial distrust of each other and began the process of living together, they soon found that to preserve the peace, each had to make some logistical concessions.

Now Miss Mattie kept her laptop computer in her study/office/guest room. It was on a long wooden table alongside the printer and her telephone answering machine. She used a soft pinkish-colored chair with wheels when she used the computer, so she could roll around in her study between the table and her book-shelves. At the beginning of their current project, Dickens had quickly chosen that very chair for himself. *After all*, thought he, *I'm doing all the hard work; Shakespeare is just talking*.

Dickens' chair selection allowed Shakespeare to claim

his favorite chair, although he would never have admitted it to Dickens. It was a wooden folding chair in which Miss Mattie had put an enormous cushion. Shakespeare loved sitting in this chair; it was the place for most of his creative thinking and his very best dreams. And he didn't even mind that the enormous cushion was pink! He was quite comfortable with his masculinity, after all.

"Okay. Now, Dickens! No more of your funny business," ordered Shakespeare like a military general. "This is my story, and I don't want you adding anything to mess it up. Got it? Not even one word! What in the world are qwertzysniggleedoodums anyway?"

Shakespeare was in quite a snit because he was just plain tired of trying to coax Dickens to type for him. He had begged and pleaded for days on end. Finally, he had even agreed to let Dickens have first go at any treats their mom gave them just to get his help.

When he woke that morning, Shakespeare had thought that this might finally be the day he could get his story down on paper. (Although, how he proposed to actually print this story was another matter!) He was quite eager to get it recorded before he forgot all the details. After all, he wasn't getting any younger! He'd already forgotten most of how he even knew this story in the first place.

Today had seemed an ideal time because their mom

was out, and they had unrestricted use of the laptop. Both boys had full tummies and freshly washed faces. Everything should have been perfect. But now here was Dickens, mucking about as usual.

"Chill out, honorable brother! I'm only trying to help," said Dickens in what could be termed an almost apologetic voice. "Surely you know about qwertzysniggleedoodums. They live under the bed and make all kinds of bumping, crackling, hissing noises while you're sleeping! They hide when the light comes on so nobody can see 'em, but you sure know they're there. I remember one time when I lived with the nurse. We were all in our cages one night. It was really raining hard, and we were trying to sleep. Then suddenly—"

"Dickens!"

The shout and ensuing growl from Shakespeare shook Dickens from his reverie. One look at those green eyes caused him to reply right away.

"Okay! Okay! You talk. I type. Got it!" Dickens was muttering into his whiskers. He really did not enjoy this kind of close encounter with his unfriendly brother. Shakespeare was quite impossible to work with. Why, he had simply no imagination at all!

Hmpph! I ought to just turn this laptop off and take a nice long nap, thought Dickens. *I just wonder how he'd like it if he had to type this stuff all by himself!*

It was a good thing for him that Shakespeare could not read his thoughts at just that moment.

"As I was saying," Shakespeare continued in his deep, theatrical voice, "stories start at the beginning so that is precisely where I shall start. Type this: In the beginning there was just darkness. No lights. No fireflies. No sun, moon, or stars. No people. No animals. No vets or rabies shots or litter boxes or cat treats or creepy crawlies or flea collars or…" The words began to tumble from Shakespeare like a snowball rolling down a hill, growing faster and faster until Dickens had to put a stop to it!

"Hey, Shakes, you're getting a bit off target, aren't you?" Dickens interrupted bravely as his paws flew over the keys. It was nice being able to ruffle Shakespeare's feathers a little bit. "Mom will be home soon, and we're going to have to hurry to get it all done, or she'll catch us using her computer."

Dickens looked at his brother from beneath his great long lashes just to see what effect this statement had on him.

~ 4 ~

The illustrious Shakespeare put out his right foot and s-l-o-w-l-y licked bottom to top. Then he looked over his foot at Dickens.

"Right. Well," he said a bit sheepishly, "I'm just trying to make a point! There was nothing there in the beginning. Just me and Him."

"There? Where? Him?" asked Dickens. He turned his head, looked over his very wide nose, and said, "Who's him? You talking about your dad?"

"Well, yes, in a way," Shakespeare answered, still hard at work on that right foot. Between licks with his bumpy pink tongue, he continued, "Some people call Him Father. Some call Him God. But He's the One who was the beginning of everything! Nothing ever existed before Him, and everything you ever saw or heard of was created by Him. So I guess you could say He's our Dad."

"Gee whiz!" Dickens said quietly as he sat back in his chair to let this thought sink firmly in. "You mean I have a Dad, and He created me?" In typical Dickens fashion, his thoughts were off and running. His eyes were narrowed, but the pupils were quite large as he thought about God and his own creation—whatever that was. "I always thought I was an orphan."

"Well, indirectly," Shakespeare said, calmly at first. Then he completely lost his patience, and his voice began to rise in volume. He sat up on his haunches and popped Dickens on that soft and very wide nose. "We are never going to get finished with this if you keep interrupting. You're getting me all mixed up!"

"Sorry!" Dickens said defensively.

Anyone could tell he really did not mean it. For if there was one thing that Dickens was good at, it was asking questions. Sometimes it seemed as if Dickens really did want to know the answer. But most of the time, it was perfectly obvious that he just liked asking questions to get people all mixed up. And while we're on the subject, it didn't seem to Dickens that it took very much to get his older brother mixed up these days.

"So," Shakespeare continued with a sigh, "there we were, just the four of us, when—"

"Whoa!" Dickens typed a bit, then whirled in complete and utter amazement.

This time he turned so fast that the chair spun around. His back was in front of the laptop as he looked at his brother.

"Wait a minute! Wait just a minute. You said just you and Him. I'm not real good at math, but even I can add one and one and come up with two. Where do you get just the four of us?"

Shakespeare began to explain patiently. Well, all right then, not patiently, but just slowly. He helped Dickens get the chair right by bumping it with his head. This head-bumping thing was one of Shakespeare's little quirks. Sometimes when Miss Mattie was busy working, he would leap up into her lap and begin to bump her chin with his head; he said he did it to get her to scratch him. (Whatever the reason, this trick did come in handy for putting things back in their original and proper places before their mom came home.)

With a sigh, Shakespeare tried again. "See, Dickens. This is the sticky part, and if you don't get it right in the beginning, then nothing else I tell you will make much sense. He isn't just one person; He's three persons all in one." Shakespeare knew this was a risky explanation, but he tried it anyway.

Dickens opened his mouth wide, stuck out his long pink tongue, and gave his nose a swipe. "Oh, I get it," he said calmly. "Like that horrible thing someone brought Mom from somewhere, the one that had four heads!"

Shakespeare shook his head from side to side more than once. "No, Dickens. Not one body with three heads.

Three separate persons! God is three in one."

Dickens stopped mid-lick and said firmly, "Okay, I'm thinking I'm not hearing you right! This is getting way too deep for me, and it's not fun anymore. I can feel a good, long nap coming on."

Dickens jumped down from the computer table and purposefully walked away, you-know-what high in the air, and making ever so much noise with his heavy feet. (It always amazed Shakespeare that those tiny feet could make so much noise.) Dickens walked straight ahead and didn't even look back—not once.

"Wait!" Shakespeare whined. "Let me try to explain." He really needed Dickens to understand. After all, they'd only just begun the story. But there was more to it than just needing help typing his story. There was so much more coming that Dickens just had to get this part straight. As he sat thinking, Shakespeare had to admit that this had been a rather rough start.

When he spoke again, something in the tone of Shakespeare's voice brought Dickens back into the room. He peeked around the door at his brother.

This oughta be fun, thought Dickens with a sneer. (What? You didn't know cats could sneer? Well, that was exactly what Dickens did.)

Out in the hallway, he turned 'round in a complete circle and softly padded back into the room and over to the computer table. He sat on the floor and looked up at his brother, his head tilted to one side and his eyes beginning to narrow. He was beginning to have some doubts about being part of this project. He was also having very serious thoughts about the sanity of his older brother.

"Okay," said Shakespeare, subdued but also thinking that Dickens was seriously overreacting, especially when there were even more troublesome truths to explain in the future. "I'm gonna take this really slow. God, as I call Him, is actually three people—He's God the Father, and God the Son, and God the Holy Spirit."

Shakespeare braced himself for the outburst that was sure to come.

~ 5 ~

And just as Shakespeare had anticipated, the eruption occurred. If he thought that Dickens had overreacted before, he found this next scene barely possible to believe.

Dickens hadn't even made it back into his chair yet. "Spirit? You mean like a ghost?" He howled as if someone had just told him his you-know-what was on fire.

"Okay! That's it! Finito! The end! That's the final straw. You are nutso! You never ever told me we'd be dealing with . . . I never ever heard you mention . . . well, what I mean is . . . I've got better things to do with my free time. Get somebody else to type for you. I'm not getting mixed up with ghosts. Those things are dangerous!"

His words came in staccato bursts, like someone playing with one of those rubber balls attached to a wooden paddle by an elastic cord—Bong! Bong! Bong!

This time Dickens didn't walk or clomp away. He frantically ran out of the study, down the hall, and into the sitting room as if he were being chased by a great big d-o-g, muttering to himself as he ran: "Walk through walls, make windows break, blow the howly-growly wind on dark and stormy nights—oh my goodness!"

He pushed and shoved until he had his entire body (except for a small tip of his you-know-what) between the sofa cushions.

"I did not say ghosts!" Shakespeare yelled right back. He jumped down from his chair and slowly followed his brother into the sitting room, talking with every step. "I said 'spirit' but not like a ghost. Please give me a chance here, Dickens!"

"Oh, yeah, well that clears it right up! Big difference!" Dickens muffled voice could now be heard from the complete opposite side of the room behind the drapes. "I'm sure I get it now." You could tell he didn't mean that either.

But against his better judgment, Dickens had to admit that he was a bit curious. Slowly—the kind of slowly that only a cat can do—he came out from behind the curtains and into the room. He sat in the center of the beautiful carpet Miss Mattie had bought on one of her adventures and looked sternly at his brother for a long time.

When he thought the time was right, he started walking toward Shakespeare. He didn't even glance at his brother as he slowly walked past him and back down the long hallway.

"I will listen to what you have to say. But only listen," he said sternly.

As Shakespeare followed him back to the study, he began again, "Look, let me try to explain it in another way. Let's talk about water for a minute. What do you call it when you freeze water?"

Can a cat put his paws on his hips? If so, that is exactly what Dickens did. He froze in his tracks and looked back at Shakespeare.

Dickens huffily asked his brother, "What do you think I am, a complete blockhead?" His eyes were narrowed to fighting slits. "When you freeze water, you get ice!"

Under his breath and behind his long whiskers, Dickens was thinking that Shakespeare had finally snapped! *What in the world did this ice business have to do with ghosts?* But he kept walking back toward the study—much against his better judgment—whatever that meant for this cat!

"Right," said Shakespeare happily. When he felt that it was safe, he continued. "But it is still water, right?"

After he stared at Shakespeare for ever so long as only a cat can do, Dickens put his head down and went on. Soon both cats were slowly heading towards the study.

Stopping in the doorway, Dickens said quietly to himself, "I don't think I like where this is going."

But he jumped up into his chair and put his paws on the laptop. He clenched his pointy cat teeth, determined not to open his mouth! He stared straight ahead, refusing to even look in the direction of his brother. Of course, as most often happens, a small point of his soft pink tongue was left hanging out, making him look even less studiously interested.

"Don't give up yet. Just give me a minute," Shakespeare pleaded. "Now, what do you call it when you boil the water and the cloudy stuff comes at the top of the pan?" Shakespeare jumped into his chair, turned around twice, and sat down facing Dickens.

"Steam," said Dickens matter-of-factly with his mouth set in a semi-sneer.

He still refused to turn around and look at Shakespeare and was beginning to feel like he was taking a very poorly written science test. Even his resolve not to open his mouth faded in the light of showing Shakespeare that he did know the answers.

"Right," Shakespeare was enjoying this teaching session now. He started to work on his left foot with great determination. But while he licked and cleaned, he kept teaching. "So water is liquid, and you can drink it. It is ice, and you can put it in a glass of tea. You can boil it, and it becomes steam. But it's all water. It's just three forms. Three forms of one thing: water. See?"

"Well, yeah," Dickens said, still puzzled. He turned ever so slightly to look out of the corner of his eyes. At last, Shakespeare had begun to talk about something he could understand. But it still did not make any sense, not in the light of what they had already typed. "I get the water part. But I thought you were talking about this God guy, not water. I still don't get that," he said.

"Dickens!" yelled Shakespeare at the top of his cat lungs. The left foot was not going to get its proper bath. Shakespeare was up on all fours at this point and looking very much like he wanted to bite his brother. "Stop being so thick, and think!"

Suddenly, like a bolt of lightning, Shakespeare remembered something he had read that might help. He sat down on his hind legs and looked at Dickens. "Okay, I have an idea. Let's have a chemistry lesson."

"Oh goodie," said Dickens, most sarcastically. "My favorite!"

~ 6 ~

Shakespeare continued, undaunted, "You know that cat across the hall, Miss Lois' cat?" He looked hopefully at his brother.

Dickens was beginning to feel like a small schoolboy who didn't quite know which answer to give. He could not for the life of him figure out what that fat cat across the hallway had to do with this chemistry lesson. He turned completely around in his chair and answered very slowly while looking deep into his brother's eyes. He seemed to be trying to determine whether there was a light on in there or not.

"Mmmmm, yeah?"

Shakespeare was enjoying this teaching business and totally failed to notice his pupil's complete lack of enthusiasm or comprehension. "What's his name?"

Dickens, ever the obedient schoolboy, replied, "$H2O$?"

"Right," Shakespeare shouted with glee. "And, my dear brilliant little brother, what does that name mean?"

Shakespeare was so happy with this line of explanation and the anticipated answer that he decided to give his ears a wash.

Truthfully, and a little fearfully, Dickens answered, "Er, I don't have a clue. I always thought it was a real stupid name, but of course this cat could never be confused with one who actually had some brains."

Surprisingly, this answer did not bring a shout of protest from the grand professor. He had exactly the same opinion about Miss Lois' cat, but he was quite focused on his line of reasoning. Instead, he calmly continued both the ear wash and the conversation. "Well, Dickens, H_2O is the chemical composition for water. So concerning our fat friend H2O, Miss Lois gave him his name because he seemed to be magnetically attracted to water—whether in the toilet, the bathtub, the sink, or in her drinking glass.

"But as for our chemistry lesson, you should know that two molecules, or two parts, of hydrogen and one part oxygen is the recipe, if you will, for water." He sat back, confident that this time he had explained it well.

Dickens sat for a long time, staring at his brother in thwarted anticipation. His mind was completely and totally a mass of spaghetti, all tangled in knots and impossible to separate into any single thread of understanding. In the space of just a few moments, they had gone from ghosts to water to the fat cat across the hall.

What in the world did any of this have to do with anything? Finally, though he well knew it was dangerous, he ventured a comment. "Yeah, and…?"

Watching Shakespeare having an ear wash had given Dickens the same idea. He set about cleaning his very delicate ears while waiting for Shakespeare's explanation, which likely promised to be tedious.

Breathing deeply through clenched jaws and trying hard to control himself, Shakespeare began again to explain for what felt like the umpteenth time, "The chemical composition for water, the liquid form, is H_2O. The chemical composition for ice, the solid form, is H_2O. The chemical composition for steam, the gas form, is H_2O. If water can have three completely different forms, and all three forms are still water, then why can't God have three separate forms and all three still be one God!"

He paused a moment to let this sink in and observed Dickens skip a few licks in his ear bath.

Shakespeare continued, "The Father part of God stays in heaven—that's what He calls His home. He has a massive throne there, and it is grander than in any other king or queen's palace. The Son part came to earth in an earth suit—human form—but that's a later story. And after the Son went back to heaven, the Spirit part came to stay on the earth. But all three parts are one God!"

Dickens was quiet for a few seconds, trying to let this

information sort out the mess his brain was in. He was quiet, but he still continued his washing up. Finally, he spoke.

"I see," said Dickens as he gave the idea some serious Dickens-type thought. He turned his head from side to side as if he were trying to see something on the opposite wall.

Then it came. "So was it the ice part that stayed in heaven or the water part?" He paused in his washing up as he asked this, leaving his tongue hanging partly out of his mouth, giving him a rather silly look.

"Dickens! I simply cannot concentrate if you are going to keep playing these idiotic games! I promise this will clear up later . . . much, much later."

Shakespeare was losing patience with his brother's silliness. He curled his body up into a tight ball, as tight as a cat could curl with such a saggy belly. His head was down, ears forward, and it was quite obvious he was very angry!

"Sorry. Really, I am sorry. Please continue," begged Dickens, who by now was more confused than ever. He sat up and tried to look alert and ready for action. If only Dickens had known that this would prove to be some of the easiest things to understand in Shakespeare's story, he would have quit while he was ahead!

Shakespeare sensed Dickens' eyes on him. He sensed

no typing was forthcoming, so he turned his giant head in the direction of the eyes. At that moment, the keeper of those eyes spoke.

"Wow, Shakespeare. I never gave it much thought before but . . . where did you come from? How old are you anyway? Did you have a mother?"

The senior but smaller cat moved not a muscle, except for a twitch of his whiskers, and answered, "All in good time, my fine fellow. All in good time." He slowly stood, turned round twice, and said while yawning, "I think I need a nap. We'll finish this later."

Shakespeare's yawns were fearsome to behold. His bottom jaw went down, and his top jaw and head went up. One could see all the way down his throat; it was a terrifying sight, to be sure.

One wonders if he really were sleepy or just exhausted from trying to explain this new concept to Dickens. Whatever the reason, Shakespeare returned to his curled-up position, yawned again until his jaws popped, then closed his eyes and went right to sleep.

Dickens had to hurry and close up the computer because he could hear the key in the lock. Uh oh! Miss Mattie was on her way in. He just had time to snap the lid shut and put his paws on top when she walked in.

"Oh, Dickens, you are such a cutie pie," cooed Miss Mattie. "You are always sleeping on my keyboard.

Someday I'm going to have to teach you to type."

Dickens mumbled to himself (which sounded a lot like purring to Miss Mattie's ears), "Oh, Mom, if you only knew!"

~ 7 ~

Early the next morning, after Miss Mattie left for work, the two cats jumped up on the computer table.

"Now, Dickens, where were we?" asked Shakespeare as he turned round and round in his chair before finally settling down. One would think he couldn't remember how much trouble he'd had the night before.

"Let me see," replied Dickens as he read over the words he'd typed last. "Oh, yes. We were doing the water, steam, ice thing."

Dickens couldn't believe how calmly he had just said those words. Honestly, he doubted he'd ever look at water the same way again. After just having a few slurps from their water dish, he'd had the silliest dreams imaginable the night before.

"Ah!" said Shakespeare with a groan. "My headache is coming back. Why in the world did I ever think I could work with you?"

"C'mon, bro! Let's get on with it. Mom will be back in a few hours."

"Okay," said Shakespeare, against his better judgment. "Read me the last thing you typed, and there better not be one word about qwertzysniggleedoodlydoodums!"

Even though Shakespeare was deliberately messing up the name of one of his favorite nighttime critters, Dickens calmly read him the last few lines that had been typed the night before. He could already sense that this day was going to be a repeat of the day before or maybe even worse.

Gathering his thoughts while scratching under his chin, Shakespeare began again. "Yes, well, so there we were in the dark. Well, no, that's not quite right. Wherever God is, it's light because He is light. But when we left heaven, everything we stepped into, everything around us, was dark. Does that make sense?"

"Kinda," answered Dickens as he typed. "I'm not too sure where you're going with this but just keep on for now."

Dickens' paws flew over the keyboard. Suddenly he stopped typing and turned to Shakespeare. "Say, brother of mine, did you ever tell me exactly how you got involved in this story?"

In spite of himself, Shakespeare found himself actually entertaining this question with a small degree of interest. His eyes narrowed as he put all his brain cells to work, trying to remember. "No, I don't think I did," he said. "And I'm not really sure I can explain it. All I know is . . . well, um, I . . . I just sort of knew that something was going to happen, and I didn't want to miss it. I wasn't actually invited, you know. I just sort of tagged along. When I saw God walking, I quietly ran along beside."

Dickens interrupted this roundabout answer. "So there are cats in heaven?"

Shakespeare was indignant! "What do I look like, a potted plant?" he asked with fire in his eyes. "Dickens, do you want to hear this or not?"

Ooooh, what a question! It took every ounce of discipline Dickens had—which didn't quite add up to a pound—to answer positively. He thought he was being rather polite with this answer. "Sorry. I just thought—"

Shakespeare cut him off angrily. "Well, how many times do I have to tell you, my fine fellow, don't think! Just type!"

The fine fellow in question had quite an attitude by this time, but he decided it would save some fur if he just gave in. He was murmuring and scratching his nose furiously, but he didn't actually say a word.

"We all stepped out of heaven together and into this really black space. You know how it is when it's so dark you can't see your paw in front of your whiskers?"

"Yeah, now that is something I can finally identify with," Dickens said. He had stopped typing and was watching Shakespeare closely, very closely, in fact. Shakespeare noticed this rapt attention and thought perhaps he was finally getting somewhere with his brother. But then Dickens opened his mouth and proved him to be completely and totally in the wrong.

"Hey, Shakes. Did you know you have more whiskers on the right side of your face than on the left?"

Shakespeare felt his blood pressure rising, but he determined not to let Dickens know. He gave himself a quick face wash and counted to three thousand and sixteen (or thereabouts) and then said, "Since that unscientific and totally unproven observation has absolutely nothing to do with our task at hand, I shall ignore it and continue." He looked up toward the ceiling as if asking for divine guidance, sighed, and closed his eyes briefly.

Dickens really was trying hard to concentrate. It was just such a difficult thing for him to do. He would jolly well rather be chasing moths or eating than typing this stupid story. But he just could not figure a way out. So he mumbled and grumbled to himself, building up quite a case in his mind, which made his eyes cross in such a comical way. He stopped mumbling just long enough to stick his long pink tongue out, lick his right paw, and give that sore ear a quick wash.

Meanwhile, the older and ever so much wiser cat knew he had missed something in his explanation of a perfectly understandable event in history, but he wasn't quite sure just what it was. Nevertheless, he slowly and cautiously (and quite a bit stubbornly) went on with his story.

"Well, it was that dark and then some. Even my extra special cat vision didn't work in that blackness. If it hadn't been for the light all around God, I wouldn't have been able to see one thing! I stayed very close to Him though—cause I couldn't tell if we were stepping off into a hole or something."

"Wow!" said Dickens. One really never knew how those circuits in his brain were connected and just what it was that lit him up. He stopped typing and looked over at his brother. "Now that must have been some kinda dark. What kind of flashlight did He use?"

"Flashlight?" demanded Shakespeare. "Who said anything about a flashlight?" It was becoming increasingly hard for him to stay in his chair. He kept trying to lie down, but every time he found a good position, Dickens said or did something that called for him to stand at attention!

Sheepishly, Dickens said, "Well, I just thought—"

"And I thought I told you not to think!" Shakespeare was losing his patience again. His voice was at a feverish pitch, and his whiskers were sticking out in all kinds of odd angles. His back was arched and that stump of a you-know-what was fluffed up like a cedar tree. He looked so frightening that Dickens quickly abandoned whatever else he thought of saying.

"Okay. Okay. I'm typing!" He turned back to the keyboard, muttering under his breath, and put his paws over the keys—ready and waiting!

Trying to keep himself focused and trying even harder not to lose control of his remaining senses, Shakespeare continued. "We stepped out into this really black space—black and empty feeling—like a cave. Now, first I need to say that wherever God is, there is light—lots of light. Everywhere He goes, things get brighter just because He is there. But this place was dark and empty. And God's light wasn't shining yet—behind Him, yes. But in front of Him, not yet. It was like—"

Dickens interrupted bravely, "Like he's wearing an invisibility cloak?"

Shakespeare decided not to glorify this ridiculous comment with a reply and calmly continued, "And God just said, 'Light, BE.' And all of a sudden there was light like from hundreds of floodlights, blinding, bright light. It was really, really bright!" Shakespeare was staring at the wall as if he could actually see into that long ago time. "My eyes hurt from the fast change from black to white. In fact, it was light like God's home is light. But it happened so suddenly that it seemed the words had hardly come from His mouth and then there was no more darkness."

~ 8 ~

Shakespeare watched Dickens' furry paws flying over the keyboard and wondered how he had really managed to get more than two sentences in a row out of his mouth without interruption. In an instant, the thought flew through Shakespeare's mind, then right out again when he noticed that Dickens had stopped typing. He turned around in his chair to face his brother, and the spell was immediately broken.

"Awesome!" Dickens said. "How did he do that? He took off his invisibility cloak? Magic? And he just said 'BE?'"

"Magic?" Shakespeare now seemed to be crying. Actually, it was more like whining than a cry. "Haven't you been listening to me, Dickens? This is God we're talking about. God does not do magic. He's bigger than magic. He doesn't need tricks. He just is! And when He speaks, stuff happens. And yes, He just said 'BE' but in a big booming voice."

Suddenly, Shakespeare had what could only be called

a revelation. "Dickens, you know that voice Mom uses when we're in trouble? She just uses one of our names and says it so loud and serious? 'Dickens?' You know what I mean?" He noticed Dickens listening very closely so he quickly continued, "Now don't go thinking God was saying the light was in trouble, but that's how He spoke—loud and serious."

Dickens decided it might be best not to say anything in reply, so he just meowed softly and kept typing. Shakespeare took this as a sign to continue. Then suddenly, another thought came to him.

"Dickens, remember that TV show we watched with Mom last night?" Dickens slowly turned and faced his brother. He said cautiously—very cautiously—"Yeah, kinda."

Shakespeare continued, "Do you remember how it began? The TV screen was so black that Mom wondered if her picture tube had gone out."

Dickens perked up at this comment. "I do remember that—and I wanted to ask Mom what that meant. A picture in a tube? I mean—"

Shakespeare interrupted this line of thought. "Stop it, Dickens. Do you remember what happened next?" Before Dickens could even open his mouth, Shakespeare continued. "It was a totally black screen. And then, something opened—it's actually called a curtain—and out stepped a person. As soon as he stepped out, one big light was clicked on. Remember?"

"Yeah, sorta," said Dickens. In truth, he had begun a nap because the TV screen was so black.

"In the theatre, that one light is called a 'spotlight.' And if you'd been awake for the next part, you would have seen the actor talking to the audience in the spotlight for a second and then all the lights in the house were turned on. And each person could see the one sitting next to them. Understand?"

The first thought in Dickens' mind was that the word *understand* might be a foreign language. But, he quietly said, "Not really. What does this have to do with—"

Shakespeare interrupted. "Dickens, I am trying to connect something you actually saw with your eyes to what happened that night long ago. We stepped out of our light world—heaven—into something very, very black. When He stepped out of heaven, it was like a spotlight on Him—wherever He walked, there was light. But when God said, 'Light, BE,' it was like when they turned on the house lights. All around us there was light. See?"

When Shakespeare saw that Dickens was quietly trying to see this in his mind, he cautiously continued.

"God named the light *day*, and He called the dark *night*. And He really liked what He'd done because He said it was good. Oh, yes, all this happened on the first day."

"Uh, 'scuse me, Shakespeare," Dickens bravely interrupted. "The first day of what?" He was gazing at his brother with new eyes. This story was getting interesting! Confusing, to say the least, but it was interesting.

"The first day of time, Dickens," Shakespeare said, quite impatiently. "The first day of life. The first day of living. The first day of everything. The first day of the beginning." By now Shakespeare was up on all fours, trying to stretch.

"Oh, I see," said Dickens, though he really did not see at all. In fact, he almost decided not to ask any more questions ever again. This was surely turning into a bigger deal than he'd ever imagined. Shakespeare was acting strangely and had a peculiar look in his eyes. Plus, this story he was telling seemed just a little over the top.

"So what happened next?" asked Dickens, just to keep up the appearance of paying attention.

"Well, nothing happened that day. We were finished for the day. And we went home." Shakespeare was thinking about how quickly God had done all this creating and how very long it was taking for Him to get it recorded. How in the world had he ever thought that he'd be able to do this simple task with Dickens? It was going to take forever! The very thought of it made him sleepy.

"That's enough for now, Dickens," Shakespeare said with a long sigh. "I'm in need of a nap."

~ 9 ~

Later that same evening, after Miss Mattie left for her night class, the two cats returned to the computer table. Shakespeare felt that he needed to get a little further than just the first day since there was such a lot to tell. He did his best, but Dickens had needed quite a bit of persuading to get him back on the job. Shakespeare had to promise to give Dickens a bigger share of his nightly treat to get him to keep typing.

"Now, Dickens, what I'm going to tell you now is even a bit more confusing than the first part," began Shakespeare, a bit apprehensively.

"Oh boy," said Dickens, scratching his right ear. "I don't know how much of anything could be more confusing than that water, ice, and steam stuff." Dickens had a tendency to scratch his right ear when he was daydreaming or worried. However, this typing job was beginning to seem more and more like a nightmare than a daydream.

"Well, the only reason this part is a tad confusing is

51

that what I'm going to tell you doesn't exist anymore." Shakespeare spoke as calmly as if he were describing what they were having for dinner.

"Oh, now I see!" muttered Dickens sarcastically, scratching furiously. Dickens couldn't help himself, and his brother didn't even notice that his ear had begun to itch. Usually, the sight of Dickens scratching that right ear brought Shakespeare into fighting mode. He'd been known to screech, "Dickens, for the love of heaven, how can anybody's ear itch so much? Do you have ear mites?" But this time, he didn't even seem to be paying attention.

"So the next morning when we stepped out of heaven, we found ourselves in this wonderful, glowing, light place." Shakespeare began to look dreamily at the window. "Everything was light. Well, not quite everything because there wasn't anything there, just light."

I'm not going to say one word, thought Dickens to himself, trying frantically not to scratch. In fact, he didn't even look up. He just kept typing and patting his ear.

"God took a look at all the water and—"

"Okay, now stop!" Dickens couldn't help himself. He got louder and louder, like someone pushing the volume button on the remote control, until he was positively shrieking. "And what water would we be talking about here? The ice? The steam? The liquid? You just said there wasn't anything but light, and now you're talking about water. How is anybody going to make heads or ta—?" Dickens caught himself just in time. He began to talk a bit more quietly. "I mean, how is anybody ever going to understand any of this?"

Shakespeare didn't even seem to notice that close call reference to his you-know-what. "Just trust me on this, Dickens." He was trying his best not to lose patience with his typist who, after all, was only a volunteer, younger, and not too bright.

"There was a ton of water. In fact, that's all there was. I didn't see it at first because it had been so dark. Water was everywhere. And God separated it into two parts."

"Oh, I get it! Like the Atlantic and Pacific Oceans?" Dickens was proud that he'd finally understood something and even more proud that he could spit out the names of the two big oceans. He sat looking at Shakespeare with a triumphant look in his eyes. But Shakespeare did not take this bit of information to heart. He hung his head till it almost touched his fluffy white chest.

"No!" Was Shakespeare crying? "No! No! No! Okay. Let's try again. Imagine that you are in a huge glass bubble in the middle of the ocean. Or even better, if we tossed that silly hamster ball into the ocean."

Miss Mattie had a classroom pet named Harvey and sometimes she babysat him on the weekends. The gentlemen felines loved watching that silly thing going round and round in his cage, but when Miss Mattie took him out and put him in the ball, their ears really perked up!

"What if we tossed Harvey in the ocean and he went down . . . down . . . down . . . There's water all around, water above, and water below. You cannot see anything but water. That's how this was—just tons and tons of water." What Shakespeare was thinking at this time was a blur because his eyes seemed to be firmly crossed, and his whiskers hung limply around his twitching mouth.

"Hamster ball, I like that," muttered Dickens as he typed. Muttering always made his nose itch, so he had to stop for a scratch and a few sneezes.

"Yes, well, don't type it because we were not in a hamster ball. There was just a lot of water all around. God separated it into two parts, and He put sky in between. He spoke to that water and said 'Firmament (or sky) BE!' Looking down from heaven, all you could see was water. And looking up from the water, all you could see was sky and more water." Shakespeare feared that at this point even he was becoming confused!

Uh huh, thought Dickens, scratching his ear again. But he didn't even look at Shakespeare because somewhere in the dark recesses of that twisted Dickensian mind, he knew better than to stare at people who were a bit wonky in the head!

"Trust me, baby brother. It is all going to clear up soon." When Shakespeare spoke, Dickens turned to look at his brother and saw that Shakespeare was smiling. No, actually, Shakespeare was grinning!

"And just what is so funny?" Dickens asked, very annoyed. He sat straight up in his chair and gave Shakespeare a particularly fierce glare. At least, he hoped it was fierce because that is exactly how he felt.

"I was just thinking about things beginning to clear up." Shakespeare seemed to be staring at something on the ceiling, so of course Dickens looked up as well. He looked so far up that he nearly fell over backward. Shakespeare resisted smacking his brother and instead calmly said, "You'll understand in a few more days."

Dickens, on the other hand, was beginning to doubt if he would ever understand anything ever again! He righted himself in the chair, gave his face a quick wash—just so he would be more alert—and tried ever so hard to listen.

Shakespeare continued, "Now here's where the confusing part comes. There was a lot of water below the sky, kinda like a huge ocean. And all around what God was creating, He put a kind of shield to keep the water above from coming down to the water below. There wasn't any need for rain because this shield kept the sun from cooking things (only we didn't have the sun yet), and it also kept the part below the sky moist and protected like in a greenhouse. It was the most perfect plan ever."

Oh, was Dickens scratching now! He didn't understand much of this at all. But he decided that it was prolonging his misery to keep asking questions, so he just typed with his left paw.

Shakespeare, of course, knew that Dickens didn't understand. He knew it was confusing, but he didn't know any other way to explain it.

"Trust me, Dickens," said Shakespeare in the kindest voice imaginable. Then he had an idea. "Hey. Let's think about eggs for a minute."

"No, I don't think so, Shakes." Dickens shook his head sadly. "I'm still chewing on the water part."

"I mean it, Dickens. This is waaaaaaaay out, but it might help you understand what I'm trying to say. Think about an egg. You've seen Mom crack them open before, right? There's a yellow middle that is called a yolk. And it is just floating in that white part, right? So what if this egg were tossed in a tub of water? Think about the sky being the white part and the water being the yellow part. God put a shell around the whole thing. See? Water, sky, shield—or eggshell—floating in more water." Shakespeare was so proud of himself because he had explained this so well. He thought the egg thing was a stroke of genius.

But the noise that Dickens made as he ran off the table and out of the study was not the noise of someone who understood things. It sounded more like a scream of terror. When Shakespeare went to see what had happened to Dickens, he found him huddled in the corner of the kitchen, furiously scratching both his ears!

~ 10 ~

"Dickens!" shouted Shakespeare. "What in the world is wrong with you?"

"Nothing that a nice long vacation from you wouldn't fix!" Dickens answered firmly.

"Come on! I told you it was confusing. The reason you can't understand it is because this shield thing isn't there anymore. That's why we're having so much trouble with weather and things now."

This got Dickens' attention. "What do you mean it's not there anymore? What happened to it?" He stopped scratching for a short while and followed Shakespeare back into the study.

The two brothers got settled into their usual positions. Shakespeare knew he was on shaky ground, so he tried to make his voice soothing.

"Ah, my dear little brother, that is another story entirely. Let me just say that these things happened on day two. God separated the water. He called the area in between sky, or some people say heavens, and then He put this protective shield around everything He had made."

"Okay." Dickens forced himself to talk, even though he knew he had better just type. "You said you guys came from heaven into this blank, dark nothing, right?"

"That's exactly right," answered Shakespeare, glad that Dickens had finally quit scratching and begun to concentrate. Oh yes, he'd noticed him having a go at that silly right ear—he'd just exercised his incredible willpower and refused to comment.

Dickens continued, "But now you say that God called the part He stuck in the middle of all the water heaven. Whassup with that?"

"No, Dickens!" He was getting annoyed in spite of himself. "God lives in heaven! That is different from sky. There are actually three heavens; it seems nearly everything with God comes in threes! There's the sky, where the clouds are. There's the heaven, where the, well, you'll see that tomorrow. And then there's the heaven where God lives. Some people call the sky heaven, because they have figured out that heaven is up, but that is not the heaven where God lives. Nobody knows where that heaven is except God and the people who are there with Him already. Got it?"

Shakespeare really hated to mention that part about the clouds because he was afraid that Dickens would want to know where the clouds came from, and that was just too much like another science lesson. He was having enough trouble explaining the creation of the sky to even imagine how he would ever explain cloud formation!

Thankfully, Dickens was too exhausted to worry about clouds. And, as usual, he was hungry. As he closed up his typing station and walked to the food dishes, Dickens thought about those clouds. He loved watching clouds—those white fluffy ones that sometimes looked like fish or birds or eggs. Where did that come from?

He shook his whole body from head to the tip of you-know-what, then turned to his brother and opened his mouth to ask about those clouds. Instead, he yawned. Shakespeare took that to mean all was well, so he too started for the food bowls.

While munching on their food, the cats were a study in colors. The golden orange cat towered above his older brother and was almost double in size. But even from the back, there was something almost regal about the black and white one known as Shakespeare. The two of them looked so, well, brotherly.

The peaceful scene was soon broken by another one of Dickens' annoying habits. Every morning, Miss Mattie put out two bowls full of food for the boys. It didn't seem to make any difference to the cats which one they ate from; in fact, both of them seemed to like munching from each bowl at different times of the day. But it made little difference into which bowl Shakespeare put his nose, for that was sure to be the bowl Dickens wanted! He would shove his big head into the bowl Shakespeare was munching from and begin to eat. On any given day, this happened more than once, and Shakespeare merely moved to the other bowl.

But this day, Shakespeare was hungry and tired—mostly tired of dealing with his brother. He stuck out his hefty white paw and planted it firmly on the side of the bowl from which he was eating. Then he muttered, "Dickens, I would think twice about what you are attempting to do. Go ahead—make my day!"

Dickens wasn't too sure what that meant, but from the tone of voice his brother was using, he guessed it might be serious. So he put his head back in the bowl he had been eating from and continued to munch. While he munched, he was deep in thought—as deep in thought as was possible with Dickens.

Day two felt like day two hundred to Dickens. He was beginning to wonder just how many more days he was going to have to listen to before life returned to normal!

After their evening snack, both cats set about having a good wash. One wonders why a cat must wash its entire body from ears to you-know-what just because it has eaten a meal! Each one stretched slowly—stretching out first one long front leg and then the other, while putting his head up in the air and stretching his whole body. It was quite a production, to be sure. It rivaled anything synchronized swimming had to offer.

One at a time, each cat jumped up on their favorite yellow chair and curled up tightly together. Soon both cats were dreaming—Shakespeare about the wondrous creation story he had witnessed, and Dickens about eggs in hamster balls floating in steamy ice!

~ 11 ~

Quite a few days passed before the cats had a chance to get back to work on the story. The interruption was caused by the arrival of the maid. Miss Mattie had a part-time maid and cook named Ida Pearl, and when Miss Ida came, no one could do anything! She stirred up such a racket that both cats ran for cover under whichever bed was closest.

Miss Ida had her own ideas about how things should be done, and she did not appreciate being told that those ideas were wrong, thank you very much! Miss Mattie and Miss Ida had had quite a few loud discussions over the years about how Miss Mattie wanted her house cleaned, arguments Miss Mattie usually lost. Actually, it seemed that she knew from the start that she was going to lose the argument, but she fought valiantly nonetheless.

Miss Ida was the tallest, widest woman Dickens had ever seen, and loud and not particularly fond of felines. She didn't work in their house every day but just came in on the weekends, which was quite a relief to the cats.

They always wondered if she had a family or any pets of her own. If she did, she never once talked about them, at least not with the brothers present. Shakespeare thought this was very strange. Dickens thought everything about Miss Ida was very strange.

Dickens was especially terrified of Miss Ida's vacuum cleaner. If the truth be known, Shakespeare didn't like it much either, but he never let on to Dickens how frightened he was. He put on a good show of courage and valor on the front lines of battle whilst he dove under the nearest piece of furniture and forced himself to go to sleep. Dickens, however, was not fooled. He was quite aware that this machine of terror was as frightening to Shakespeare as it was to himself. In truth, he was saving that knowledge for a time when he could put it to the best use.

This particular day had turned into quite a trying time for our author and his scribe. They were just getting ready to get back into their story, when they heard Miss Ida at the door. They always knew when their mom was near because they recognized her footsteps. With Miss Ida, it was another story. She whistled in the hallway, so they could hear her coming from a long way off. But today she wasn't whistling, and they were taken by surprise!

They just barely had time to close up the laptop and

leap off the table to the sofa when Miss Ida walked in. They were sitting on their backsides like very guilty bookends, but of course, Miss Ida didn't notice. She didn't even speak to the cats. In fact, she rarely did. She just kept walking and went right to the kitchen to start to work, which was a loose interpretation of the word when it concerned Miss Ida.

Miss Mattie had told her over and over that she wanted things moved in the flat before Miss Ida dusted and cleaned the floor, but the cats knew she never did it. Miss Mattie also wanted Miss Ida to shake the rugs and vacuum and mop underneath them each week, but she never did that either. Both cats snarled at her whenever they could to let her know they didn't approve. Most times she snarled right back.

Sometimes Dickens thought Miss Ida knew what he was thinking. Today was one of those days. He was just stretching his back like all cats do when Miss Ida came into the room with her dusting things. "Shakespeare," he murmured under his whiskers—which, remember, sounded a lot like purring—"how much do you bet she doesn't shake the rug?"

"Don't say one word there, Mr. Fancy Pants," Miss Ida said to Dickens. Sometimes the names she called a fellow could really grate on his nerves! He wasn't wearing one single item on his whole body that even remotely resembled trousers! "You just keep your furry little mouth shut tight. I'll get this cleaning done as I always do, and nobody needs to tell me how to do it! No rug worth its salt needs to be shaken every week! The very idea!"

Shakespeare opened one eye wide at this comment. Miss Ida saw it and whirled around and addressed him. "And I don't need any advice from you either, Mr. High and Mighty!"

Oh, this woman could be so exasperating at times! Shakespeare had not said one word, not even one little whimper. High and mighty indeed!

Dickens and Shakespeare thought maybe Miss Ida must have had a rabies shot or had her temperature taken before she arrived—that always made them a bit mad at the world! She really was in a foul mood today about something.

She banged and clanged the pots and pans in the kitchen until a gentleman could hardly concentrate on his newspaper. By this time, Shakespeare was sitting on the computer table in the study, trying very valiantly to read the headlines in the *Wall Street Journal.* He could not keep his mind on his reading with all the racket, however, so he just gave up and stretched out for a short nap.

When she started up that terror machine, both boys thought it was time for a nice long sleep and put all thoughts of writing history to rest for the day. Oh, how they wished their mom would come home and deliver them from this horrid woman! What in the world had they ever done to her to make her hate them so? She was most definitely a mystery and a source of never-ending misery to our two usually calm (and always spoiled) gentlemen.

~ 12 ~

One could certainly not say the house was clean as a whistle, but one could most definitely say the house was quiet. Too quiet.

Shakespeare yawned, sneezed, and stretched all at the same time, as only a cat can do. *Finally, we can get back to work,* he thought. Raising his voice, he directed his attention at his sleeping brother. "Come on, Dickens. Wake up!"

Snoozing on the keyboard, Dickens was having a wonderful dream that had not one thing to do with the peculiar story his brother was telling him. It felt good to get all the muddle out of his brain and sleep soundly for a while. He really didn't want to wake up. He twitched his whiskers and rolled over on his back, exposing his ample white tummy to the sky. What a mistake!

Shakespeare strolled over, a cat on a mission. He stopped right beside Dickens, opened his mouth to the proportions of a small shark, and clamped down on a juicy bite of furry fat!

"Eeeyeow!" shrieked Dickens in a mixture of shock, pain, and fury. He fell to the floor with a thud and rolled into a protective ball. "What is the matter with you? What are you, a cannibal?"

Shakespeare explained through clenched jaws, "Miss Ida is gone, and we need desperately to get on with things before Mom gets back." If you have never seen a cat with clenched jaws, you have missed a frightening spectacle.

The tender-bellied and badly insulted Dickens knew enough not to argue with Mr. High and Mighty. So he reluctantly abandoned his napping place. After a yawn and a stretch, he slowly, oh so slowly, quite nearly slithered around the computer table (not once but twice) and finally came back to his place at the laptop.

"I am not amused, Dickens!" snorted Shakespeare through rigid white whiskers. "If you don't want to help with this, just say the word, and I will do it myself!"

His ears were set at a frightening position. Dickens knew he was in for a real clobbering, but he still couldn't resist hitting below the belt—that is, if cats wore belts.

"Oh, now that would be something rich to watch," chortled Dickens. "Your feet are two sizes bigger than mine; you'd never get as much as one line typed!"

Dickens knew that he had hit his mark. You see, neither cat had claws in their front feet in order to protect Miss Mattie's draperies, clothing, and legs. But

Shakespeare won the prize for the saddest story because his first surgery had been done when they lived in a country where this operation was not so commonly performed.

It was a sore spot with Miss Mattie that she had paid quite a lot of money and put Shakespeare through a great deal of pain and then found that he still had his thumbs. He was able to do a considerable amount of damage to her yellow chair before she could have those thumbnails removed. As a result of this operation, he had very large feet. Long, slender legs with soft, white, pink-soled, enormous feet!

Dickens, of course, got in on the more expert claw removal, so his feet were nicely shaped, even if he was the larger cat. His toes could fairly fly over the keyboard, something Shakespeare had to admit he could never accomplish.

Now lest you be one of those individuals who think declawing is a horridly cruel operation, let it be known herewith that neither of these feline gentlemen was ever allowed outside. They did not need to climb trees, fend off ferocious Dobermans (perish the thought), or dig in the dirt to hide their droppings. And most everyone knows, of course, that cats don't claw furniture to tear it (most of the time), but in order to stretch their feet and leave their scent mark on the furniture. Their soft front feet were still capable of all the things cats do (like bopping brothers on the head, cleaning ears and faces, and even climbing on the furniture) without shredding the draperies, sofas, or legs.

Indeed, Dickens was quite proud of himself for getting this latest arrow straight to Shakespeare's pride. *It's about time he realized how valuable I am to him,* he thought with a snarly glance over his shoulder. *He started all this anyway. My tummy will never be the same!*

And just in case you think that the size of his feet never bothered Shakespeare, rest assured it did. He was very well aware that this was an enormous obstacle to his desire for self-sufficiency. He was extremely jealous of Dickens' prowess at the computer and had recently taken to hovering near Miss Mattie when she worked just in case he could pick up a tip or two. He seemed so attentive, purring contentedly, that Miss Mattie had been heard to comment, "Shakespeare, if I didn't know any better, I'd think you were proofreading my work." (Little did she know!)

The older brother in the family felt it best to make an attempt to smooth this quarrel before it got any bigger, so he got up as if to stretch himself, padded across the table to his younger brother, and gave him a quick lick or two across that extra sensitive right ear. On any given day, these two were either rough and tumbling through the flat and wreaking havoc as they went, or they were lying quietly like two contented peas in a pod, giving each other a good wash. Shakespeare had hopes this tactic would work, and it did.

- 13 -

And so, their brotherly spat in a timeout, the two eventually got back to work. "Where were we?" demanded Shakespeare, already forgetting his vow to be nice. "It is becoming most impossible to remember things when I am interrupted so many times."

Dickens dutifully read back the last few lines. He had cleverly discovered a way to save their work on Miss Mattie's hard drive in a specially coded Windows file, so she never even noticed it was there.

Maybe Shakespeare had had a more colorful life and witnessed some major miracles, but Dickens felt that he was surely no slouch in comparison. He knew a few things about the computer after all, much to Shakespeare's dismay.

However, right now, Dickens was feeling quite ill-used. His feelings were hurt, which one could certainly tell by the downward slant of his usually perky white whiskers. Shakespeare chose to ignore the attitude problem going on in the almost orange cat. He relaxed a bit in his chair and began to move his thoughts back through time.

"This is a day you are really going to like, Dickens. Lots of wonderful, exciting things happened. Are you ready to type?"

Taking his life in his paws at this point, Dickens braved yet one more question. "Shakes, before we get into a new day, I was wondering if you'd try again on that water thingy. I'm still not quite settled as to why there has to be three gods."

Surprisingly, Shakespeare took this as an honest-to-goodness question and did not lose his temper. He sat gazing at his brother, deep in thought, while his mind rewound the tape of the previous conversations. Dickens thought maybe Shakespeare was going into some kind of trance because he was quiet for so long. But for once, just this once, the typist wisely refrained from talking.

"Okay," began the professor in a few more seconds, "let me try again. You and I have three parts. We have an outside part that everyone else can see—our bodies. We have an inside part that has to be X-rayed to see—our bones and muscles and tissues. And then we have our thinking parts, our emotions, the part that even an X-ray can't reach. That part is called the soul and nobody yet has ever been able to figure out where it is! Okay so far?"

Dickens nodded, though he'd never thought about

himself like that; it did make sense. Still, he was a bit nervous about where Shakespeare was going with all of this.

"I'm trying to say that if we can have three distinct parts and be just one cat person, then what is hard to understand about God having three distinct parts and being just one God?" Shakespeare thought this explanation a bit wobbly, but it was the best he could think of on the spur of the moment.

Why did Dickens have to make everything so hard? If he, Master Shakespeare, could understand and accept this concept, what the dickens made it so hard for—

All of a sudden, the light came on. Shakespeare knew now what the problem was. Dickens was trying to understand God with his brain, to see the answer, so to speak. Anyone who knew Dickens for more than five minutes could understand the difficulty of him trying to understand any sort of concept with his muddled brain! Anything, of course, other than food, shelter, and those confounded butterflies he found so fascinating.

Across the small room, Dickens had no idea of what was going on inside his brother's head. He was busy trying to sort out a tangle in the pad of his right foot. Gnawing and chewing and biting and licking just didn't seem to move that knot, but he kept at it nonetheless. When he realized that Shakespeare had stopped talking, he turned to look at his brother.

Shakespeare was staring at Dickens as though he'd never seen him before. Or as if he'd like to not see him anymore; Dickens wasn't sure which. As he gazed back at Shakespeare, Dickens felt he could almost see that light bulb go on inside; he really could! "What's up, bro?" he asked fearlessly.

Shakespeare looked almost kind and gentle, and this really made Dickens nervous. "Listen to this one thing, Dickens," he began slowly. "Have you ever heard the word *faith* before? And do you understand what it means?"

Dickens stopped working on his foot. He answered slowly, "I think so. Maybe. Umm, well, I guess not."

"Well, there's a book Mom reads, the Bible, and it is all about faith. It says that faith is believing something we can't see or really understand, just believing it is true." Shakespeare watched Dickens to see how this concept went down.

"Say what?" Dickens had stopped chewing completely and sat upright to face his brother. "How can you believe something you can't see? That makes no sense to me at all!"

"Exactly," began Shakespeare. "It didn't take any faith at all for you to sit in that chair, did it?" Noting Dickens' calm acceptance of what he was saying, the senior cat continued, "But if I pointed over there and asked you to try out that soft new blue chair, what would you say?"

Dickens knew exactly what he'd say, and he said it. "You're nuts! Sit in a chair that's not there? Shakespeare, you might think you're trying to help, but I'm more confused than ever! I started this conversation asking you to explain that water, steam, ice thing, and now you're talking about chairs I can't see!"

"I am trying to explain the water, steam, ice thing, Dickens! I am just saying it takes faith to . . . Okay. What about this? Let's get back to three parts. If I peeled off all your fur, would you still be Dickens?"

Dickens looked as though he were going to bolt, and he was remembering that previously mentioned crocodile bite to his soft middle parts. He shuddered from his ears to the tip of his you-know-what and then said, "I surely would hope so! But you better be sure that if you try anything like that, I'm going to fight back!"

Shakespeare felt he was entering very troubled waters, but he continued. "And if somehow we could take out all your bones and inner parts, would you still be Dickens?"

Though positive that his elder brother had been sniffing Mom's supply of catnip, Dickens' answer was delivered in a calm gentleness that he certainly did not feel. "I don't think I know."

"Okay, then I've explained this badly. Let me try again. If you have bones inside your body—that's kinda like the Jesus part of God; He's the flesh and blood part.

If you have a thinking part that can't be seen—that's kinda like the Holy Spirit part of God. He helps us to do the right thing by helping us think good thoughts and understand what God wants. And the Father part of God kinda ties it all together, holds it all in—like the skin and fur on your body. See?"

Dickens most certainly did not see. In fact, he was so confused that his whiskers hurt! He was thinking very strong thoughts about just what to tell his teacher about his modern teaching methods when Shakespeare interrupted.

"Oh, Dickens. You've just got to get this; you cannot understand all of this with your brain. You've got to know it in your 'knower'—by faith! It's just impossible to try and sort it out by seeing, tasting, touching, feeling, hearing. If you will just trust me, it will all make sense as we go on with the story. I promise."

Shakespeare felt as if the wind had been knocked out of him. He just had no more energy to go on. He lay down on his soft pink cushion, put his enormous head down on his wide paws, and closed his eyes. He felt a good, long cry coming on.

~ 14 ~

Shakespeare might have been thinking of a good cry, but all of a sudden, the light went on in Dickens. He fairly shouted, "Shakes, I know! I know! I know! It's like the qwertzysniggleedoodums! I can't see them, but I know they're there. Is that faith? Huh?"

Slowly but surely, energy began surging through every part of Shakespeare's body. He sat straight up in his chair, looked across the room at Dickens, and joyfully (okay, not joyfully, but surely more happily than a few moments before) said, "Yes, Dickens. If that is what it takes for you to understand faith, then it is surely true! You strongly believe in the existence of doodleesnigglums or whatever you call them and have never actually seen one. That is faith!

"But another thing I thought of just now—you know how the sun comes up every single morning, no matter what? You know that it's out there even if the sky is cloudy and dark, right?"

Dickens' eyes were round and he had the silliest grin

on his face. "I never gave that much thought before, big brother, but I guess you're right."

"Well," said Shakespeare slowly—he was actually thinking on his feet as he'd heard his mom say so many times. "That's faith. You can't do a single thing about that sun shining in the sky—but when we go to sleep at night, we have faith to believe that in the morning, the sun will be shining. See?"

Shakespeare could tell by the look on Dickens' face that he did see. So, he cautiously continued, "Although most times you can see Mom fill up our food and water bowls, you also just know that she's going to do it, right? That's another example of faith."

"I think I'm beginning to see that this faith stuff happens in more places than I'd ever thought about before," Dickens said slowly.

Shakespeare was grumbling in his whiskers and thinking to himself that only an idiot would believe he could catch a red fish on a television screen, but Dickens was going to start believing now that this was another example of faith. He'd surely have to straighten all that out before the important things came along. "And now can we please get back to our story?"

"Aye, aye, captain," said Dickens as he tried to salute. He only succeeded in bonking himself in the head, however, and that did not help him very much. Blinking ever so slightly, Dickens tried to focus on the laptop screen. And there was another thing. Shakespeare said he had to know in his "knower." *Wonder where that is*? thought Dickens. *One of these days, I've got to ask.*

Pretending not to notice Dickens' current dilemma, Shakespeare began, "Okay then. So on this day, God stepped out into this beautiful sky blue, umm, well, for want of a better word, I'll just say sky. It was the most beautiful color I'd ever seen this side of our home in heaven. And then, right before our very eyes, He collected all the water underneath the sky into one place. And then he spoke, 'Dry land, BE!' And from out of all that water, dry land appeared."

"Say what?" Dickens was still a bit muddled and had been typing almost on autopilot. But this statement grabbed his attention. "Land appeared outta water?"

"That is exactly what I said, Dickens," replied Shakespeare excitedly. "This was something to watch. Everything everywhere was water, all over the place. Now, I know that you've never been on a ship in the ocean, but if you had, you'd know what I mean. Water all around; all you can see is water in any direction. Sky above and water everywhere else. God just put His hands out, spoke 'BE' and out of all that water, land appeared. We were waaaay up in the sky, so what I was seeing looked like those pictures the astronauts sent back from space, only different."

"Oh, now that makes perfect sense," said Dickens in a huff. It seemed like he was back where he started when they began this confounded typing job. This day was not turning out any better than the ones before. "Same but different. Just what is that supposed to mean?" As he sighed, Dickens sagged his shoulders a bit till he seemed to be lying right on the keyboard.

The larger, younger cat felt that Shakespeare was forever trying to make him feel like the poor relation, to put him in his place as the second man in. How dare he bring up that you've-never-been-on-a-ship deal? Of course Dickens had never been on a ship; he was an indoor cat, for heaven's sake. And another thing: how did he know for sure that Mr. High and Mighty had ever been on a ship either? The saggy body was attached to a very alert head that now turned to focus on his brother. His eyes narrowed to small black slits.

Seemingly unaware, Shakespeare continued as if talking to a small child. "Something happened much later to change how the land was formed, dear little brother. But I'm trying to tell this story in a logical order and not jump around from place to place. See, the pictures the astronauts send back from space are different because the earth is different now than it was when God made it."

"Hold on!" Dickens was wide-awake now. Paws off the keyboard, he turned to face his brother. "You saying

God made the earth?" Dickens knew this word because Miss Mattie had a beautiful, mostly blue globe in the sitting room. Sometimes she sat touching it and spinning it around, looking at all the beautiful stones that decorated it. When she did this, Dickens sat spellbound, waiting to see if she would sing. And sure enough, nearly every time, Miss Mattie would start singing Dickens' favorite song, "He's Got the Whole World in His Hands." He loved it when she got to the verse that said, "He's got the puppies and the kitties in his hand." He tried to sing along many times, which always made his mom laugh out loud.

Suddenly, Dickens' memories of fun sing-alongs with Mom were jerked back into the present by the growling voice of his brother.

"That is just what I have been trying to tell you, Sir Blockhead! God called all the water He gathered up *seas*, and He called the dry land *earth*." Shakespeare had so much more to tell Dickens about what happened on that day, but he was feeling completely exhausted about then. He suggested they take a short break and have a little snack.

~ 15 ~

After a snack and a short catnap, the two brothers returned to the laptop. They certainly had a most unique work schedule. They didn't interrupt their work for breaks; they interrupted their breaks for work.

Shakespeare finished a quick wash and began where he thought they'd left off. It was mightily hard to tell lately where one had started and where one had stopped. But he tried valiantly to gather his thoughts and keep to some semblance of order.

"God looked over all that He had accomplished with this water and land and pronounced it good," he began. "Now comes one of my favorite parts. He held out His hands, and talked to the earth. And things began to grow from it: trees with fruit and trees without fruit and plants and grass and flowers. But Dickens, get this—no weeds! Not one bad thing was in that earth; it was all good.

"God made things with seed inside. The trees had fruit on them, all the right kind of fruit. I mean, the apple trees didn't have peaches on them, and the peach trees didn't have pears on them. Everything grew just as God intended for it to grow. And it looked so beautiful! God said this part was good too. It was the end of the third day."

Dickens was typing as fast as his paws could fly. He really wanted to ask some questions, but this story was getting really good. He was a little afraid that if he got Shakespeare sidetracked again, he might suggest they stop for the day, and then he'd miss something important. *They were really on a roll,* he thought. And then it happened.

Shakespeare continued. "Dickens, now you remember that shield or hamster bubble I told you about?"

Dickens began to feel the walls closing in on him. He was having trouble breathing. His right ear was beginning to itch. His whiskers were twirling around in circles. *Here it comes,* he thought, *bubbles again!* He must have fainted because the next thing he knew, there was Shakespeare bonking him in the face with his big fat paw and fairly shouting at him.

"Come on, Dickens. Quit playing around! Really, now this is getting totally out of hand!"

"Sssorry," said Dickens, shaking his head and trying hard to focus. "You were saying?" His eyes were still a bit wonky, but he sat up and tried to get his paws on the keyboard.

"I was saying," said Shakespeare in a very controlled voice, "that now you are going to find out just what I meant by that shield." Honestly, Shakespeare was questioning his own sanity at this moment. This exasperating little brother of his was totally and completely out of hand!

"Oh, yeah," said Dickens, still in a fog, "the shield." He couldn't help himself. He reached his paw up and started to pat his right ear.

Shakespeare went on without even seeming to notice that Dickens had stopped typing with his right paw. "Well, there were rivers and lakes everywhere. All this beautiful green stuff did not have to be watered because their roots were down in the ground, and the ground had water in it. Of course, there was nobody on this earth, just plants and trees. But if there had been anyone there, that person would not have had to do a thing. There were no weeds, and nothing needed watering."

"No bugs either?" asked Dickens. He said this because a moth flew by right about then, and he wanted to stop and chase it. Dickens did love a good chase. And since his head was still spinning and his ears were ringing and his eyes were not quite focusing, he couldn't help thinking that this might be an excellent time for a break. However, it quickly became evident that Shakespeare did not share that view.

"Of course not! Just plants and trees. Are you paying attention?" Shakespeare hadn't noticed the moth, so he didn't realize that Dickens was absent without leave from his post. Without looking toward him, Shakespeare shouted in the direction of his brother, who by now was seriously involved in the chase for the moth. Shakespeare's voice was at an almost feverish pitch.

"I told you God made everything good and perfect. The rivers kept everything watered from the bottom up. Then when the water began to evaporate, the shield around the earth would cause the evaporation to turn into a mist, watering everything from the top down. Now was that a great system or what?" Shakespeare began to feel almost confident that at last Dickens would understand.

If truth be known, in spite of himself, Dickens was finding this story really interesting. He forgot all about the moth, and it happily flew out of reach. He hopped back up to the laptop and began to quickly type out what his brother had just said. Try as he might, he couldn't stop the words from coming out. "You know, Shakes. I think I'm beginning to get this bubble deal. Like the shell on the egg protects what's inside, right? The shield protected what was inside from whatever was outside. I think I'm getting it."

"Good!" Shakespeare smiled. "And that is just exactly how God ended this day, day number three. He looked around at all he had done and said it was good!"

And with that, another day in the cats' lives had also come to an end. Miss Mattie's footsteps could be heard in the hall, so the boys had to hurry and close up the laptop. When she opened the door, she found her two favorite felines cuddled up on the sofa. Two sets of sleepy eyes looked at her when she came into the room, and two sets of ears perked up when she said the magic word.

"Treat!" sang Miss Mattie. Two tired but happy kitties soon snuggled up beside their mom for a cuddle and a well-deserved treat.

~ 16 ~

The next sunny Saturday, two well-fed and very spoiled members of the Davis family were stretched out in the sun on the balcony of their flat. Miss Mattie was in the dining room working on a writing project and had shooed the cats outside. Their heads were very close together, so they could whisper without their mom wondering about their conversation.

"You know, brother of mine," began Dickens, "I've been kinda wondering about something." Dickens was lying on his side, legs straight out in front, you-know-what elegantly curled around his backside.

"What's that?" Shakespeare asked dreamily. He loved being on the balcony, especially in the sunlight. The tiles felt cool on his tummy. He was stretched out in what Miss Mattie called his seal pose: front legs folded back under his chest, body stretched to its longest, back legs and you-know-what pointing rigidly straight out. He really did look like a seal, well, except for the lack of front flippers and that beautiful black and white coloring.

"How come is it that God made this earth and all this green stuff and there wasn't anyone to take care of it? I mean, where were the people and the cats?"

"All in good time," Shakespeare said with a yawn. "All in good time. You see, God is really interested in order. He wanted to get everything all set before He put living things in. That's why He got the earth all perfect and beautiful first. Sorry, but you'll just have to wait a bit to find out the rest."

Dickens had actually asked a very good question this time, Shakespeare thought. *Maybe he was starting to grow up after all.* Soon the sleepy green eyes were closing, and the feline seal was fast asleep and snoring.

Shakespeare's nap was rudely interrupted by his mother's voice. "Look, boys. I've brought you a surprise."

Shakespeare and Dickens sleepily looked in their mother's direction, fully expecting a food reward. But it was not a cat treat. They were horrified to see what she had for them—a huge, fat ball of fur called H2O.

Miss Mattie didn't seem to notice the lack of enthusiasm amongst her little family. She opened the sliding glass door wider and gently tossed the fat feline outside. "Miss Lois is having her flat sprayed for bugs while she's out shopping, so we're going to babysit H2O. How's that for a surprise?"

Shakespeare and Dickens felt sure that the bug spray

would have been a better choice for that tub of cat lard than their having to put up with him all afternoon, but because their mother was watching, they moved over to let H2O have a place in the sun.

Miss Lois was a teacher in their mom's school and had just moved into the flat across the hall. She really loved Miss Mattie's boys, so they tried to love her back. They were making really good progress too, until she got her baby. She was so silly over that ball of fluff that it made Shakespeare and Dickens quite ill. H2O was not only enormous; he was also quite plain. His coat was plain black, and his eyes were plain brown. His whiskers were plain white, and his expressions were plain boring. Shakespeare and Dickens felt him a plain handful to have to tolerate. Really, he had no interests in life at all except eating, sleeping, and water!

Miss Mattie was always kind to her neighbor, but she drew the line at letting a cat with front claws have access to her furniture and drapes, to say nothing of her legs. So all three cats had to share the balcony for their Saturday morning nap. Two of the three were not a bit happy about this arrangement. The third member had just noticed the bucket of water sitting under the air conditioner to catch the drips.

Faster than anyone could have thought, H2O was in that bucket. He had begun by watching the drips from the air conditioner, looking at them with those round (though plain) brown eyes, which were quite crossed from being too close to their target. He watched for a time, and then he began to try to bat the drips onto the sleeping Davis boys.

After several unsuccessful attempts, he decided to try to catch the drips with his tongue. This was what led to his downfall. For when H_2O put his huge paws on the edge of the almost full bucket, he lost his balance and fell in the bucket. Of course, the howling and hissing that erupted, combined with the flood of water quickly approaching them, woke Shakespeare and Dickens. The balcony wasn't quite large enough for three howling and very wet cats, but they had no escape. There was such a lot of water and noise! Miss Mattie ran to their rescue but not soon enough.

The worst part of the whole thing was that this entire bucketful of water ran straight down the drain hole on Miss Mattie's balcony and right onto her downstairs neighbor's clean laundry. The previously friendly neighbor was surely not happy with the dirty rinse water and lost no time in telling Miss Mattie so.

~ 17 ~

Later that afternoon, the intruder was back in his own flat, the Davis boys were dry from their spontaneous, unwanted, and unexpected bath, and the balcony was sparkling clean. Miss Mattie apologized profusely to her downstairs neighbor and offered to rewash his laundry, take it to the professional laundry, or pay for new clothes. Things were serious when she offered to buy something new to replace a damaged item. Miss Mattie was famous for her thrift and for her creative ways to recycle, but she also knew it could be tedious to live upstairs from a furious downstairs neighbor. After the conversation with her neighbor, she quickly left to go out with her friends.

Her departure cleared the way for the brothers to get back to work. Dickens opened the laptop, found the file, and read the last few lines to Shakespeare.

"Okay, brother. This is a day you are really going to like." Shakespeare couldn't help himself. He just loved teasing his little brother. "Some things near and dear to your heart were created this day."

"Oh, boy!" said Dickens. "Fish! I knew it!"

"Not fish. Come on; let's get to work. All you ever think about is food!"

That was quite the understatement. In truth, Dickens felt that it was his personal good work that kept the cats well fed. Miss Mattie fed her boys a special dry food for adult males. She had devised a clever method to keep creepy crawlies (as she liked to call them) out of the cat food. There were two shallow bowls on the floor that Miss Mattie filled with water. Into each of the bowls, she then set a smaller bowl full of cat food. Her idea was that any creepy-crawly who tried to get the food would drown in the water. The funny thing was that it worked! Nothing but cat noses, sharp pointy teeth, and long white whiskers ever even got near those bowls of food.

But because neither of the cats liked dipping their delicate whiskers down into the bottom of the bowl, they much preferred to have them brimming with food. So Dickens was the alarm to let Mom know it was time to fill the bowls.

Another reason Dickens kept so focused on his stomach was that every night before bedtime, the boys got a special treat of gourmet cat food, but only a tablespoon each so they wouldn't get too fat. Miss Mattie would lead a little parade of meowing voices with upright, parallel, waving, umm, you-know-whats into their own special room (which doubled as the extra bedroom/ office). There, she set the food down on the floor, patted each furry backside, said good night, and then closed the door firmly! This usually took place between 8:00 and 9:00 p.m.

However, Dickens had been known to place himself smack in front of his mother as early as 7:00 p.m., belly on the floor, legs and feet firmly tucked, staring at her unnervingly. When she got up for a drink, to answer the phone, or just moved to have a stretch, he went into action. Singing, howling, turning around in circles— nothing was beneath the dignity of this little beggar. It never worked, however, because Miss Mattie was a very strict disciplinarian when it came to bedtimes, unless, that is, the boys had been particularly trying during the day. Then their bedtime could come as early as five o'clock!

As chief reminder, our Dickens had a unique way of announcing that he felt it was time to eat. Actually, he sang when he meowed, a bit like a soprano in a choir. And he just kept increasing the volume until one would think the end was near! Miss Mattie had been known to have a patience snap and actually raise her voice a few levels when Dickens sang, especially if she were talking on the telephone or trying to hear the evening news!

In a similar manner, Dickens particularly hated it when his mother went on a long trip. Oh, not because he missed her, oh no. It was because he missed his nightly routine. Usually, in the summertime, Miss Mattie took her long holidays abroad, and then their Auntie Jo came to take care of them. She stayed in the flat and took really good care of them. She loved to read, and Miss Mattie's library of books always made her stay pleasant. And since Auntie Jo's mom lived around the corner, she didn't mind staying over at the Davis flat one bit. The boys really loved her, but she didn't do the bedtime routine like their mom. They had become very accustomed to this nightly ritual, so visiting aunties just didn't fill the bill.

And now here was brother Shakespeare accusing Dickens of thinking of nothing but food! Really, now! After all he did for his brother, Dickens quite fairly resented the ill treatment he was receiving.

~ 18 ~

Oh my goodness. How in the world did we get so far off course? Oh, yes, Dickens and the food! Let's rejoin the cats.

Shakespeare was trying to get the story back to where they had left off. "Remember, Dickens, that I told you God is especially orderly?" he asked his brother, quickly forgetting how close he'd come to offending his best typist.

"Yep, I remember that part," said Dickens, still a bit touchy after being yelled at.

"Well, what do you think? He did something next that is very like what Mom does when we move into a new place."

"You mean he set off bug bombs?"

Shakespeare decided that the best plan of action was to just ignore his brother's ill-chosen remark and continue with his narrative. He quickly washed his face with his fat left paw and plunged back in.

"Mom always sets the furniture in place, and then she

decorates the walls with pictures and pretty things, right?" asked Shakespeare in a tone that could only be called insulting.

"Oh yeah," said Dickens. "That! So God hung pictures?"

"Dickens!" hissed Shakespeare. "Are you deliberately trying to fry my noodles?" Shakespeare was using an expression that his mother often used when talking to Dickens. He had always thought it a rather odd expression, but now it seemed to fit perfectly.

The orangish cat was extremely pleased with himself. But he put on his most innocent look and turned his round and not-so-innocent golden brown eyes to his brother. "Not at all, Shakes. I'm just trying to understand. I wasn't there, remember?"

Shakespeare didn't buy the innocent look, but he did soften his tone a bit. "I mean that after God had the water and land situated and all the beautiful trees, flowers, and plants in place, he did a bit of decorating. Remember I told you about those three heavens? Well, God put something in the second one. Now we can call that heaven space.

On this day, he filled that part of heaven and space with little twinkly lights. From where we stood, they looked just like the teensy little white lights Mom puts on the Christmas tree. Only the lights God used really weren't so little if you could see them up close. In fact, those twinkly lights are actually e-nor-mous stars."

"Oh, boy," said Dickens. "I do love stars!" This was completely true. This cat loved to sit in the window at night and look at the stars. He thought they were winking at him, and when a star fell, Dickens took it quite personally. Sometimes he would spend hours looking at something he thought was a star, waiting for it to fall, only to be disappointed when the star was turned off at daybreak! He never could understand why streetlights had to be made in the same shape as the stars!

"Two of these lights had special jobs," continued Shakespeare. "One was made the ruler of the day, and the other was the ruler of the night. Can you guess what I'm talking about?"

"The sun and the moon? God made the sun and the moon?" Dickens asked with a little more enthusiasm than Shakespeare thought necessary.

"He surely did. And He put those stars in places in space with just as much care and attention as Mom puts into arranging her pictures on the wall."

"Really?" asked Dickens with his eyes open wide. "Why?"

"Two main reasons," Shakespeare explained. "The first one is that He put them in space to mark time. There were no calendars or clocks then, so the stars and sun and moon were set up to mark the beginning and end of days, weeks, months, and years."

"Wow!" said Dickens. He was really impressed! This water, steam, ice guy was quite the builder and designer! He had no idea that somebody had actually made the sun, moon, and stars. In fact, Dickens reckoned he'd never even given a thought to where they'd come from. For a brief instant, he contemplated asking what they were made of, but just as quickly, he thought better of that idea. He was ever so curious and filled with anticipation for what his brother would tell him next.

"But another important reason is something that I can't completely explain right now," said Shakespeare cautiously. He knew this was going to send Dickens off into orbit again. But Dickens was so busy typing that he forgot to ask any silly questions. So Shakespeare continued very carefully.

"You know how Mom likes to put special things on the walls and then explain what each thing is when people come over?" Shakespeare asked.

As he typed, Dickens nodded his head, so Shakespeare went on. "Well, God had something special He wanted to tell about how and why He put his stars in space, so He arranged them in a pattern. He was planning to tell a very important story."

"Yeah, but, I mean, like, who was He going to tell it

to?" asked Dickens. "Nobody was there but you guys, and I'll bet you already knew this story, right?"

"That's right. And that is the part that you're going to have to trust me for and wait a bit. I don't want to tell you yet because I am trying to tell this story in order as it happened. So for now, let's just leave it by saying all these things happened on the fourth day."

"Aren't you forgetting something, big brother?" Dickens asked.

"Hmm?" said Shakespeare, who was already thinking about a bit of dinner. In anticipation, he lowered his body close to the ground, getting in position to relieve some very tired muscles. His stretch started low, then went high, then went out—really quite something to see were Shakespeare's stretches.

"You left out something pretty important."

"I most certainly did not," Shakespeare answered indignantly. "How would you know anyway? You weren't there!" It was most annoying to be interrupted mid-stretch.

"Well, for the last few days you've been telling me that when God finished making something, He said—"

"Oh! I did forget! How clever of you to remind me, little brother," Shakespeare interrupted. "God said that everything He had done this day was good! Day four."

He jumped from his chair and headed for the kitchen

and a well-deserved meal. Meanwhile, back at the laptop, Dickens was what could only be called thunderstruck. *Shakespeare called me clever,* thought Dickens. *My, that surely makes my day good!*

~ 19 ~

Several days went by before the feline historians could get back to their work. Dickens could hardly wait to hear about the next day of creation because Shakespeare had promised him that something brilliant happened on this day. He was never quite sure what Shakespeare meant when he said that b-word. Sometimes it was something wonderful; sometimes it was something that Dickens had done rather stupidly. But somehow Dickens felt that this time it was going to be the former usage rather than the latter.

So after a nice bit of lunch and just before his ever sleepy eyes got too heavy to be able to type, Dickens hopped up on the table, opened the laptop, and shouted for Shakespeare. "C'mon, big brother. I'm ready to type. Let's get on with the story!"

"I am coming, little one. Half a second." Shakespeare was busy having his morning bath and needed just a short time to finish his, ummm, you-know-what. He took particular care in grooming this part of his anatomy because it was so short. Dickens never spent too much time on his long, luxurious you-know-what for some reason. But maybe because so much of it was missing, Shakespeare spent a looong time getting every hair in place.

When finished, Shakespeare stretched himself and walked slowly (so as not to appear too anxious) to his thinking chair next to the table. "Where were we?" he asked, as always.

"Day five," said Dickens excitedly. "What happens on day five?"

"Oh, yes. This is a most exciting day. Well, now, just like the Master Builder He is, God has put everything in readiness for this day. He has the water ready. He has the land ready. He has the sun and moon and stars ready. He has the grass and plants and trees and flowers ready—"

"Aaaack!" Shakespeare's opening speech was interrupted by a shout from Dickens. "Ready for what? Get on with it!"

"I am, Dicksie," said Shakespeare with a bit of a growl. He did so hate being interrupted when he was waxing eloquent! He certainly knew that God had not suffered any interruptions when He was creating the world. Of course, God did not have to create the world with Dickens around, now did He?

"The next two days are the most important ones of all. It is exactly like when Mom moves us into a new place. She gets the floors cleaned and shined. She moves in the furniture. She hangs the pictures. She gets all the groundwork, so to speak, finished first. And then she brings us!"

"Cats?" Dickens said rather too loudly. "We're getting cats today?"

"Almost," Shakespeare said quite impatiently. "If you will just hush and let me think!"

"Sorry! I'm just trying to stay focused!" Dickens was tapping his right paw on the edge of the table in a most annoying way.

"Yes. Well, so am I, so stop that!" said Shakespeare. "Okay, so the land is ready and the sea is ready. And on this day, God spoke to the water and out of it came everything that lives in the sea—yes, fish! He made the teeny tiny minnow and the great big whale. He made crabs and lobsters, starfish and seahorses, and every kind of swimming thing imaginable. He made the octopus, those long slithery things called eels, and even the jellyfish."

"Wow!" Dickens was really interested now! "Did you get to taste one?"

"Oh, Dickens! You are such a twit! Of course I didn't taste one! God was creating not cooking! Will you let me finish? For once in your life, will you try not to think about your stomach?"

"Go on. Go on, please! This is really getting good."

Dickens couldn't help himself; he was really trying to type and soak it all in at the same time. In some opinions, Dickens was one of the most genuinely trying individuals ever known.

"After He made all the sea creatures, God looked up into the sky. He spoke to it and out of it came everything that flies—birds, insects—all of it. He sorted them all—I mean the water creatures and the sky creatures—into groups so that they could have families. And then He told them all to get busy and have babies and increase their numbers. It was a sight to behold. All the color, all the flapping of wings, all the splashing and slurping from the water—wow!"

"Oooooh, I would love to have been there to see that. Birds and fish—two of my favorite things!" Dickens seemed to be drooling as he typed.

He was ever so fond of birds and fish. If Miss Mattie left the television on a nature show, he would sit as if hypnotized, watching only the birds and fish. He really didn't care much for lions and tigers and elephants and creepy crawlies. He had even been known to stand up on his hindquarters and bat at the screen when a particularly noisy red bird appeared.

In the country where they lived, one of the television stations had a videotape that ran every morning just before the regular programming began. There was a camera set up in front of a small aquarium full of colorful fish. Shakespeare could not count the times he had strolled into the sitting room to find Dickens watching the fish as if for the first time and focusing on a brilliant red fish. He could hear Dickens mumbling to himself, "This is the day, Red Boy. This is the day I am going to have you for my breakfast." Dickens would tell Shakespeare that he knew it was only moving pictures, but the elder, wiser brother had serious doubts about the truth of that statement! And what was it about red that seemed to attract the younger cat, anyway?

Dickens stopped typing as a thought hit him. "But wait. God must have made more than one of each of these birds and fish, right? Else how could they get busy making babies?"

"Well, one would suppose that to be the case. Actually, He made lots of males and females. They were adults too, not babies. And at the end of this rather long day, God did it again. He said it was good! He was pleased with what He had done."

Shakespeare was also quite pleased with how well this day had gone with his brother. No major catastrophes or completely idiotic questions. At least so far.

~ 20 ~

Dickens finished typing the last sentence and then looked studiously at his brother. "Say, Shakes," said Dickens. "Can I ask just one teensy weensy little question?"

Against his better judgment, and with whiskers twitching in a curious sensation of alarm and distrust, Shakespeare nodded his head. So Dickens began. "You said God created the things in the sea and the sky, right?"

"Yes, Dickens, that is exactly what I said," Shakespeare answered him quickly.

"Well, I kinda want to know, errr . . . what did He make them out of? I mean, you said God held out His hands and said 'BE' and there was land and then trees, plants, flowers, and stuff. So what about all these things? How did He make them? From what?"

"Dickens, that is one of the best questions you've asked so far. And the answer is, I don't really know." Shakespeare knew this was not the answer Dickens was hoping for. "I didn't see Him holding anything in His hands. One minute there wasn't anything in the sea, and the next it was full! Same thing for the sky."

"Um, you said the sea was full," Dickens said hopefully. So far Shakespeare wasn't losing his temper, and that really surprised Dickens. "What about the rivers and creeks and lakes and ponds?"

Two in a row, thought Shakespeare. He answered Dickens as if they were at last on the same intellectual level. "Everything happened so fast, but lakes, creeks, ponds, rivers, and seas all had creatures in them too."

"Really?" Dickens thought this was completely unbelievable! "Did God start with the big things or the small ones? I mean, did the whales come first or the goldfish?"

At this point, Shakespeare was getting a bit worried. He did not want his young assistant to lose confidence in him, but the truth was, he wasn't sure if his memory were failing or if he had been having a nap when some of this creation happened. Truth be known, he just didn't know!

He searched his memory bank for a good answer. Not finding anything satisfactory, he decided to try a sort of game with his inquisitive little brother. "I'll tell you what, Dickens. Let's try to figure this out ourselves. What would you do? Would you start with the big things first or the small things first?"

Dickens was thinking hard and for the first time seemed to be really focused. He closed his eyes and sat so still that Shakespeare thought he had fallen asleep.

"Weeelllll," he said after a long pause. "I think I'd start small and work up. That way I'd know how much room I had left. And if anybody got hungry, the little ones surely couldn't eat the bigger ones while I was busy working on the next thing."

"Logical," said Shakespeare. "Completely logical. I'll tell you what. This is a question that I just cannot answer. I know what I think, but I don't really know what happened exactly. Let's save this question for you to ask God when you see Him."

"Say what?" Dickens let out a loud whoop. "I'm going to see God? When? Where? How? Which one?"

"All in good time, little brother. Right now, let's have a nap and dream about fish and birds, shall we?"

Dickens wanted to know more, but the thought of dreaming about fish and birds was just too good to pass up. So after saving the file and closing up the laptop, the boys settled down to do just that.

~ 21 ~

The nap turned into an afternoon sleep. Two very heavy heads looked up when their mom came in and just barely woke up for their dinner that night. The next morning, though, things began to heat up very fast!

Holy smackers! thought Shakespeare, borrowing another favorite phrase of his mom's. *If it had taken God as long to create the world as it's taking me to get it all written down, He would have still been waiting for His day of rest!*

Actually, today's interruption was completely the fault of Master Shakespeare, so he had nobody else to thank or blame. The trouble began because of a rather ordinary clock.

Next to her bed, Miss Mattie had a pretty baker's rack. It had shelves that were like the racks inside an oven, meaning things placed on those shelves could be sort of wobbly at times. Miss Mattie had a rather peculiar clock on the second shelf. It was peculiar because her flat was full of beautiful, unusual, and sometimes expensive things. But this was a silver-colored travel alarm clock with very large digital numbers that glowed in the dark when she pushed the button on top. With all the lovely things in Miss Mattie's flat, one wonders why she had this kind of clock in her bedroom.

The reason was that Miss Mattie was also a very practical woman. She loved to travel, and she just never saw the point in having both a travel clock and a regular clock at the same time. It made things simpler to use the travel clock both at home and when she traveled, don't you see?

The negative for this positive was that Shakespeare had an unbelievably magnetic attraction to this clock! With all his refinement and sophistication, Shakespeare should have been the kind of cat who was above petty mischief. But this clock always seemed to woo him into trouble. It demanded his attention. He felt compelled to jump up on the bed, stretch himself to the longest possible length, reach out a fat, furry paw, and smack that clock off the shelf to send it flying across the floor.

After the clock had been put in its place, Shakespeare would have a quick wash and then return to his favorite spot on the sofa for a nap, happy with his day's work. Dickens said he just liked to see time fly, which was such an overused statement that it never failed to make Shakespeare snarl and spit. Of course, this was exactly the reaction Dickens was hoping for.

So on that fateful day, while Miss Mattie was in the

shower, that great black and white hunter Shakespeare crept into her room, jumped up on her bed, and began to stalk his favorite prey. The major complication that day, however, was that Miss Mattie had left her favorite glass on a thin cork coaster on the very same shelf.

This glass was a frosty purple, long-stemmed, crystal one that Miss Mattie's daughter had given her for her last birthday. Miss Mattie just loved to take it to bed with her, full of sparkling water with a twist of lime. This was her favorite nighttime ritual, and it really made her feel loved and special to drink from her pretty glass (note the use of the word *was*)!

You can probably guess what happened next. Shakespeare put out his paw to knock off the prey . . . errrr . . . the clock. The clock wiggled and wobbled, and then the glass started to wobble as well. And then came the crash! As the clock flew off the shelf, that lovely glass split into hundreds, maybe even thousands, of tiny little splinters!

Oh, boy. Shakespeare was really going to get it this time. Miss Mattie usually just laughed and shook her head when she picked up the clock, the batteries, and the cover from the floor. But this was a totally different matter! The great clock stalker ran like a frightened rabbit into the guest room and dove under the bed, trying his best to hide far into the dark corner.

Sure enough, when Miss Mattie came out of the shower, singing her favorite song, she was smiling; that is, until she walked into her bedroom. When she saw that beautiful glass in splinters all over the floor, she started to scream and shake and cry all at the same time. Her voice and her mannerisms became quite similar to Miss Ida's. It was a most terrifying spectacle!

"Bad boy! Oooooh, Shakespeare! You have done it this time! Bad boy! Where are you? You cannot hide from me. I could just pull you limb from elbow! Come here; I mean it! Come here!" Miss Mattie certainly had some rather peculiar expressions, to be sure.

Shakespeare was cowering under the bed, every muscle and hair on his body trembling. He knew he was in serious trouble. Oh, why couldn't he leave that stupid clock alone? What in the world was the fatal attraction there anyway? He knew better; he really did!

And then, horror of horrors, out came the terror machine. Now even Dickens scrambled to hide. Up to this point, he had been enjoying the show, but now Miss Mattie wasn't singing anymore. In fact, she was steaming. She first swept up all the pieces of her favorite purple glass, tears streaming down her face. Then she tossed them into the trash bin with a groan and used the vacuum sweeper to pick up all the remaining slivers of her treasured birthday gift. All the while, she was talking to herself—something about laying up treasures on earth where cats can knock them off and smash them.

The next thing they knew, the cats were locked up in their room (without even a tiny morsel of their usual nighttime treat), and then Miss Mattie was gone! She went to buy a new clock—one that wasn't wobbly and one that was electric. The boys thought they heard her say something about her grandfather too!

Dickens gave his brother a fierce lecture for his actions. Of course, it was all motivated by anger that he had been punished and deprived of his food when (just this time) he had not done anything wrong! Shakespeare sat under the bed, all his whiskers drooping, his ears flattened on his head, his eyes cast down to the floor. He was so ashamed—not of knocking off the clock, of course, but of his clumsiness in knocking off that blasted purple glass.

So much for writing this day. It would have to wait until Miss Mattie cooled off a bit. The cats didn't even dare to approach the computer table when she was in such a foul mood.

Another really peculiar thing happened later that same weekend. Shakespeare might have imagined it, but when Miss Ida came to clean and cook, he could have sworn she actually smiled at him! Now what was that about?

~ 22 ~

Shakespeare just wasn't his usual bossy self for days after that clock and glass incident. He lectured himself about giving in to temptation, about being weak, and about setting a bad example for his baby brother. *If only Mom had not left that blasted glass on her shelf,* he kept thinking. *So, actually, it wasn't my fault at all. It was all her fault for not putting the glass away!* Somehow that seemed to soothe him, at least a teeny bit.

Miss Mattie had come home with a huge and quite heavy electric clock, hoping it would have absolutely no attraction for Shakespeare. Of course, not understanding why he was attracted to the small clock in the first place, she had set her mind to find a clock he wouldn't have such an affinity for. Naturally, she thought of something that didn't require batteries. Her pride in being frugal went out the window in her quest to tame this savage beast. One would have to hope that the beast in question had learned his lesson, but it was extremely hard to tell with this temperamental cat.

At any rate, his pride was severely wounded, and he kept finding excuses to stay away from the laptop and anything to do with the story he had been telling. Dickens asked every day, in fact, several times a day, all to no avail.

In addition, Shakespeare wanted nothing to do with his usual pastimes of chasing spiders or watching birds through the wire on the balcony or trying to catch his mother's feet when they were unprotected. He was completely and totally not himself, rather pouty, thought his younger brother.

But then, one day, Shakespeare awoke, truly inspired. All thoughts of clocks and purple glasses gone from his memory, he felt confident that he had the hardest day ahead of him yet. Knowing his brother so well, Shakespeare had this assurance that Dickens was really going to be naughty with day six.

But still, it had to be done. This was the most important day of all the days of creation, and it just must be done right. So Shakespeare watched for the perfect moment when Dickens was full, rested, and alert—not an easy threesome for the golden boy. At last, the moment came when Shakespeare felt all systems would be go.

"Dickens, old chap, are you feeling in the mood for some typing?"

Well, finally, thought Dickens. *When he is good and*

ready! Why I ought to refuse to type another word. That would show him good and proper!

But then Dickens began to think about how if he quit typing, the story would never get finished, and for once in his life, Dickens was curious about something that had nothing to do with food! He really wanted to know what else his pompous older brother had in that hard head of his.

So he jumped up on the table, opened the laptop, and looked expectantly in the direction of his older brother. "I'm ready," he said eagerly, quite proud of being able to cover up what he had just been thinking.

"Now, Dickens," began the convicted glass breaker, "I just feel that I have to warn you. This is going to be the most important day yet. There are many things to get recorded and saved in our file, and you must pay close attention to detail. I must caution you that if you continue to interrupt me with your incessant and ridiculous questions, I will lose complete track of my thoughts, and then we will have to make unnecessary circles in order to get everything back in place. It is vitally important that you—"

Shakespeare was interrupted by a shout, most rude and vicious. "Put a sock in it, Shakespeare. I'm ready to type, so talk!" Honestly! Dickens was quite incensed by this long and overdue lecture. After all, he was doing his best to type all this unfamiliar material, and a typist sometimes needed to be able to understand what he was typing, for heaven's sake!

Oh, thought Dickens with a jolt. *Wonder which heaven that refers to when someone says "for heaven's sake!" Hmmm. If I weren't so blasted mad at him, I'd ask Mr. High and Mighty.*

On the other side of the room, our storyteller felt that he needed to tread lightly with his brother that day, so he began very cautiously. "Right. Well, then. To review, we've got land and seas, rivers and lakes, fish and birds, trees and flowers and grasses and plants, stars and sun and moon. But there is something missing. And that something is—can you guess?"

Dickens didn't even look up from his work. He murmured to himself (which sounded a lot like purring), *How dare he! Lecture me one minute and then be all cutie pie the next. Hmmmph!*

He was finished with these little games once and for all. He absolutely refused to even look his brother's way. Instead he kept his head down, eyes on the keys, completely ignoring the question-and-answer game.

"Animals!" Shakespeare seemed not to notice his brother's newfound resolve. "There weren't any animals. So on this very important day, God spoke to the earth and told it to bring forth everything with four legs. He made livestock—cows and things. He made wild beasts: lions and tigers and bears, oh my. He made domestic animals like you and me. He made lots of males and females of each animal he created. Oh, yes, and He even made the creeping things—Mom's favorite—the creepy crawlies, snakes that slithered, scorpions, and other icky things."

"No way!" Dickens could not help himself here. He had to ask. "God actually made these creepy crawlies? Hold it; that means he made fleas, right? Eeew. And in the things-in-the-sky bit, that means mosquitoes too. Why?"

"Not sure about that one," Shakespeare answered his brother. "I think lots of people question God's sanity when it comes to creepy crawlies, snakes, and especially flies and mosquitoes! But I'll tell you this: God never does anything without a purpose. People may not ever figure out what that purpose is, but everything makes total sense to God. When He finished with all these animals, He told them all to get busy and start having babies. He wanted lots and lots of animals. And it was so noisy, all of them mooing, barking, meowing, bellowing, growling—oh, but they weren't angry! Nobody fought each other. They all ate grass and plants; nobody even thought about biting another animal! Such color! Such variety!"

Shakespeare was lost in remembering. He thought of spots and stripes and solid colors, of legs and wings and fleas. He just couldn't help himself; he had to shake all over, from head to you-know-what.

"Why on earth did He make so many of each thing? I mean, just one kind of cat would have been enough, I think. But we have leopards, cheetahs, lions, tigers, jaguars—"

Dickens stopped midsentence, stuck his extra long pink tongue out of his mouth, did a long, slow lick on the pad of his right paw, and then ran his damp paw over his eyes. "Well, come to think of it, it would be kinda boring if we just had one big cat, right? And who would want the job of choosing which cat it would be? Oh, yeah, and I almost forgot. What about the Tyrannosaurus Rex? He made dinosaurs too, right?"

"You sure can ask some involved questions, Dickens," Shakespeare responded. "Of course He made the dinosaurs, and they all ate grass, leaves, and plants too. I just know that God wanted His world full of lots of variety so that there wouldn't be any reason to be bored. Animals are better to watch than television any day. Too bad the humans have forgotten that."

Shakespeare couldn't help noticing the beginnings of another series of questions coming from Dickens. He quickly stifled Mr. Curiosity with these words: "Do not even ask about what happened to the dinosaurs. I will clear all that up at a later date. I promise!"

"Okay, then, er, I suppose you wouldn't know what he made these things out of either, eh, Shakes?" asked Dickens cautiously.

"Actually, that is right, Dicksie. I was so fascinated watching all these things moving and walking—tall things, short things, fat things, skinny things, all colors and shapes and forms—I just did not pay any attention to the material He used. I have a guess about what He used, but I just don't know." Shakespeare was lost in a world of his own again, remembering the wonder of all these creatures. Of course, where Shakespeare had been living with God, he'd already seen all the animals, but they were just there when he showed up; he'd never really thought about where they actually came from. And he'd never seen them just be! This was fascinating!

In fact, Shakespeare remembered himself into a short nap.

Well! Of all the nerve! Dickens shut the laptop down and slammed the lid rather hard. "If he can do it, then so can I! And he left out the good part again!" After a few turnarounds, Dickens settled himself on the rolling chair for a short nap. He was smiling when he fell asleep, dreaming about creepy crawlies!

What Dickens didn't realize was that this was only the beginning of day six. There was more coming, lots more.

~ 23 ~

Shakespeare felt that he had just slept for a long, long time, but actually, it wasn't even lunchtime. Since their mom was out for the whole day, it seemed like a good idea to continue with the story while they could. He looked over at Dickens and found that he was stretching and beginning to wake from his midmorning nap. Good timing!

"Ready then, Dickens?" Shakespeare asked his groggy brother.

I'm going to really get him this time about that good thing, thought Dickens when he had had a stretch. Actually, he'd been dreaming about just the proper way to put it to Mr. High and Mighty. With very little thought to his own personal safety, he addressed himself to Shakespeare. "You did it again, Dunderhead!"

Smugly, he opened the laptop and found the place where they'd left off. He even managed to wobble his head a bit from side to side and smirk while so doing.

"Excuse me? Dunderhead?" Shakespeare was clueless

as to what this attack on his integrity meant. He tried frantically to remember what they had been doing, writing, or discussing before he went to sleep. Try as he might, he could not work out why his good name was being assaulted in this manner.

"You left out the good part again!" Dickens was feeling quite triumphant about this small victory over the always-right Shakespeare!

"The good part? What in the world are you talking about, Dickens?"

"You know! The part where God always says things are good."

"Ohhh!" Shakespeare began to realize at last where Dickens was headed, though he was still not quite sure about the Dunderhead part!

"Well, dear little brother, God doesn't say the good part until He is finished with His day's work. And those animals were only the beginning of day six. We've still got loads to do."

"Huh?" Dickens could not take this in. "He created everything with four legs and the creepy crawlies, and that was only the beginning? Wow, then those fish and birds must have seemed a piece of cake compared to this day, right?"

"One could suppose." Shakespeare was not at all sure how God would feel about being told that His creation of all the birds in the air and the fish in the sea was a piece of cake. But then, God already knew all about Dickens and his strange choices of words.

Meanwhile, Shakespeare was still trying to sort out that Dunderhead remark. But there was entirely too much work to be done to stop and chew on that knotty little problem just then.

"Okay. So let's just get on with things, shall we? This time I have an answer to a question you always ask," Shakespeare said. Dickens was too busy getting set up to ask, but one does wonder which question Shakespeare was referring to. After all, Dickens was known for his rapid and sometimes rabid questions, don't you know!

"After God had all the animals created and they were busy chewing grass and nibbling tree leaves, he said to the Son and the Holy Spirit, 'And now, for My masterpiece. Let's make a man just like us.'"

Shakespeare knew as he said this that Dickens was going to come unglued. And that is exactly what he did.

"Oh, boy! Hold on! Whoa! Stop right there!"

Shakespeare had never seen Dickens this upset! His back was bowed, his ears flattened back against his head, his eyes were slits of black, and every hair on his body seemed to stand at attention. He was a fearsome orange and white cat in attack position.

He turned to face his brother and forcefully said, "I

am just beginning to get comfortable here, and now you're bringing up that ice, water, steam stuff again. I think I'm getting a migraine. I need another nap."

And with that, Dickens slammed the laptop shut and proceeded to march himself to his favorite napping spot (smack on top of Miss Mattie's bed) and tried to sleep. But try as he would, he could not stop thinking about what Shakespeare had just said. When he finally did fall asleep, he had dreams of ice cubes floating in boiling water with little men on top, each one holding an egg in his hands. His whiskers jerked and twitched. The fur rippled all over his body; it was quite a sight.

Shakespeare, meanwhile, curled himself up in his little straw basket with the llama fur pillow, put his head on his paws, and smiled.

I knew it, he thought. *Just like I figured, he's losing his senses. He's going to start believing in the impossible next. Now we can get some work done!*

Shakespeare stayed curled up in his little basket for a long time, thinking about the amount of information he had been able to get onto the files in Miss Mattie's computer. He knew Dickens would eventually come around, but for the time being, he was just going to let sleeping cats lie—or however that goes.

He spent quite a bit of time in that basket, trying to decide how to proceed. Such fun things were coming.

Important and fun things. And with that happy thought, Shakespeare floated away into another nice, long nap. (Cats do sleep quite a lot, don't they?)

~ 24 ~

This time, it took many days for Dickens to settle down again. Every time Shakespeare asked him if he were ready to type, Dickens would bolt under the bed and begin to pat furiously at his right ear. Shakespeare decided to let him stew until he was ready. Meanwhile, Miss Ida came to do some spring cleaning, and that sent both cats scrambling.

Shakespeare never could figure out why Miss Ida called it spring cleaning when it wasn't spring and especially since not much cleaning ever got done. Oh, she always made a lot of noise and mixed things up really well, but the place wasn't much cleaner when she finished than when she started. This time, though, Shakespeare noticed that she paid special attention to the shelf near Miss Mattie's bed. He soon realized that Miss Ida was taunting him when she dusted that new clock.

"Nice new clock here, eh, Shakespeare, old boy? This one doesn't look as though it could go flying across the room, now does it?"

Was that a sneer on Miss Ida's grumpy old face? Though he really wanted to bite her, Shakespeare chose to ignore her crude and totally uncalled for remark. *That woman really gets my dander up,* he thought. *Like she has never broken anything! Of all the nerve!*

And so it was nearly a week later when Dickens' natural curiosity got the better of him. "Okay, Shakes," he said one day while sitting at the balcony door and looking out longingly. How he wished he could be outside watching birds instead of inside with this horrible job to do. Every few seconds, Dickens would reach up and pat his now tender right ear.

"I think I need to get on with this. I can't stop dreaming this weird dream, and I'm afraid it will never go away if I don't get some answers. Can we please just get on with your story?"

"Sure, my good chap," said Shakespeare with a smile. "I thought you'd never ask. Where were we?" Though he was eager to finish his story, Shakespeare continued to sit where he was—curled up on the yellow chair in the sitting room. He was waiting to see what Dickens would do.

"It was the man in our image thing."

Dickens' ear was really beginning to itch. He tried valiantly to ignore it. He slowly walked to the study, touching his right ear to the wall in the hallway every few steps. He hopped up to the computer table, opened the laptop, and started to search for their file.

"Okay. Now just hang on a minute, and all this is going to become clear," Shakespeare cautioned, now perched on the arm of the yellow chair. Suddenly he had a brilliant idea.

Sure, thought Dickens. *Clear as mud!*

Shakespeare trotted down the hallway and peeked his head round the door of the study. "Dickens, you know that book Mom has on the coffee table?"

"You mean that book of pictures by Normal Rockingchair?"

"Norman Rockwell," Shakespeare corrected almost patiently. "Yes, that's the one. Well, in that book there is a picture I want you to see. Come here a minute." He turned and trotted back down the hallway into the sitting room.

Dickens followed his brother as if in a trance. Shakespeare jumped up on the yellow chair. Then he leapt from the arm to the middle of the sofa where he could reach the coffee table. One wonders why he didn't just go straight to the coffee table. Dickens did.

Nevertheless, Shakespeare pushed with his nose until he knocked the book off the coffee table and onto the floor. Then he opened it with his paws. This was one of his favorite books, and he really loved looking at the pictures. He was an expert at getting it down and open, but he just hadn't quite worked out how to get the book back on the coffee table. He knew he was going to get into trouble with Miss Mattie over this, but the lesson for Dickens was most important.

He used his nose and paws to flip the pages until he found the one he wanted. "Look." He pointed with his whiskers to a picture. "It's called Triple Self-Portrait, and it's a picture of the artist painting himself, but he's using a mirror to check that he's got the portrait right."

"Relevancy, Shakes, relevancy." Dickens was using a new word he'd learned from watching old reruns of *Perry Mason*, the famous American television attorney. He wasn't quite sure what it meant, but he had an idea it had something to do with getting off track. And he felt quite sure that off track is just where his brother was at that moment. This mirror thing just did not seem to connect with either the animals and creepy crawlies or the water, ice, steam thing.

He sat on his hindquarters and tried to look interested. It was so hard for him to really focus for any length of time, but he decided to try and focus on the book. It was a funny picture, after all. Normal Rockingchair looked so funny with that long pipe sticking out of his mouth. Dickens was soon lost in wondering what a pipe smelled like and why on earth anyone would want to keep something so nonfoodlike in his mouth.

"Okay. I'm getting there." Shakespeare was trying a new tactic with Dickens but wasn't quite sure it was going to work. "Let's go to the laptop, shall we?"

As they headed back to the study, Shakespeare continued to talk. "See, God wanted to create a man in his image. I want you to get the idea of this mirror thing firmly fixed in your head. Because when I told you that God was actually three persons in one, I meant it. God the Father is the One who said He wanted to create the man, but He said 'in our image,' meaning all three parts of them in one new man."

Back up in his chair, Dickens kept his head down and his paws moving over the laptop keys. He tried not to think about what he was hearing. He did like the picture in the book, though, and so he tried to focus on how funny it looked instead of thinking about what his loopy brother was saying.

"This time, I can tell you what He made something out of, little brother." Shakespeare knew that Dickens would like this part. "It's really strange, but he used dirt to make His man, dust and dirt from the earth."

"What?" This was something Dickens just could not let pass. "Dirt? He made humans out of dirt?"

"Yes, He did," said Shakespeare quietly. "But only the first human. He stooped down, gathered up some of the dirt from the newly created earth, and fashioned it into the body of a man. Just as if He were looking in a mirror, He made this man in His image with something from all three parts of Himself. Am I explaining this clearly enough?"

"Wow!" Dickens hadn't seemed to notice, but his ear had stopped itching. This story was getting really interesting. "So God is made out of dirt? Awesome! What happened next?"

"No! God is most certainly not made out of dirt. God is a Spirit; He does not have a body like humans have!" At this point, Shakespeare fairly exploded. "Are you going to listen or just cause trouble?" He was beginning to whine like a spoiled child.

"Gee whiz. Chill out, brother! I'm just trying to follow this mirror thing. You said God made man just like Him, and if He used dirt, then I thought that logically…"

Knowing there was never any logic where Dickens was concerned, Shakespeare had to gather his thoughts once again before speaking. It seemed that in this current adventure, Shakespeare was doing much more gathering than speaking!

~ 25 ~

Shakespeare began anew. "What He used to make the human is not the in-our-image part. What made the human a reflection of God's three parts comes later. Shall I continue?"

"Oh, please. I'm more confused now than ever!" Dickens was simply being truthful and not at all troublesome, so Shakespeare made a mature decision to continue.

"Well, this is a really good part. God made this man like a little child makes an animal out of clay. He carefully formed his body—the arms, legs, toes, fingers, ears, nose—but he, the man, was just lying there on the ground. You know, like that cricket you killed once, lifeless. God somehow filled that man's body with His Spirit, and the man began to breathe and move."

Shakespeare noticed Dickens open his mouth, and he said quickly, "Sorry, don't even ask. I don't know how He did it. He breathed into him, maybe like that mouth-to-mouth resuscitation they do on the TV rescue shows. All

I know is that one minute there was a man-shaped hunk of dirt on the ground, and the next thing I knew, he was standing up and moving. Somehow, someway, God had managed to breathe his Holy Spirit part into that man. He gave the man life."

Dickens had stopped typing completely and was staring intently at his brother. He seemed to have stopped breathing. He didn't even blink his eyes. All his senses were fixed on Shakespeare. He was beyond interested; he was enthralled.

"Awesome! What happened then?" he asked quietly. The pupils of his great golden colored eyes had narrowed to tiny vertical slits, which only happened when he was angry or just about to pounce on a moth. However, neither situation applied at this time. So maybe, just maybe, he really was genuinely paying attention.

"Well, God called this man He'd made Adam. Adam had a body with skin on, like God the Son. He had God the Spirit inside of him. And he had something else—he had a soul. I'm going to explain this soul part later. Just know that Adam was an awesome creation in the image of God.

He was just like all three parts of Him. He was brilliant. He had a mind that was beyond belief. He was beautiful and perfect!" Shakespeare stopped in midthought. "Oh, I cannot wait to tell you the next part."

"What?" Dickens howled. "What is it? Don't stop now!"

"I'm afraid we're going to have to stop now. I hear Mom coming!"

Both cats scrambled—Shakespeare to get the book under the coffee table, and Dickens to get the laptop closed. They were just climbing up on the sofa to get in their naptime positions when Miss Mattie walked in. Quickly they arranged themselves in a tangle of fur.

"Just look at you two lazy boys," she said with a laugh. "What a life you have! Just lying around all day, waiting for your dinner."

Two purring, furry bodies—quite out of breath at the present moment—looked at her with wide, innocent eyes. But their minds were on one single thought. *Oh, Mom, you have no earthly idea how very wrong you are!*

~ 26 ~

It was a long, long weekend. For some reason, the thunderstorm caused Miss Mattie to decide to rearrange her bookshelves. That sent her into the closets, and she soon had all of them cleaned and rearranged. Dust was flying, and she was cleaning like they had never seen a house cleaned before. The cats never knew where she was going to be from one moment to the next so they were hard put to find places to stay out of her way. Shakespeare was beginning to think she never would leave the flat again when suddenly the sun came out.

Sunshine always made Miss Mattie think about being outdoors. Sunday evening, she decided to go out and do some shopping and then have dinner with her friends. As soon as she was in the lift (that's an elevator), Dickens was in Shakespeare's face.

"Okay, Shakes. Let's have it. What happened next?"

"Let's get the laptop opened and type it, okay?" Shakespeare was concerned that Dickens was so curious about Adam that he'd totally forgotten their purpose was to record all these events on the laptop.

"Oh, yeah. Sorry," said Dickens, and he got busy setting up his workstation. Soon he had found the file, opened it, and was ready to type. He read Shakespeare the last few sentences without his even having to be asked.

"Okay, now this is really going to get good." Shakespeare was confident that most of Dickens' confusion would be over after his next few sentences.

"So, next, God held a parade for Adam. He called all the creatures he had made—from the sky, from the sea, and from the earth—and he made them all come to Adam."

"Why? Why did God do that?" Dickens was thinking that this was about the strangest parade anybody had ever witnessed. Usually there are more spectators in a parade than participants in a parade. This one was just the other way round. He was trying to visualize a parade full of fish, snakes, elephants, cats, and fleas.

"God sent all these animals to Adam so that he could give each one a name. It was a most extraordinary experience." Shakespeare's eyes were as big as almonds as he remembered this remarkable event. "One by one, as each animal, bird, fish, or reptile went to Adam and respectfully bowed its head, Adam took but a moment to speak out the name."

"God let Adam name the animals?" Dickens asked in what could almost be called a squeak. "How in the world did Adam know what to call them? I mean, just a few minutes before he had been a chunk of dirt!"

Shakespeare thought long and hard before he answered this question, but when the answer came, it just spilled out. "Adam was the most unique individual that ever lived. Think about it, Dickens; Adam wasn't born; he was created. He was handmade by the Creator! He didn't even have a belly button. And he didn't have to start as a baby and learn to walk or talk. When he stood up from that dirt, he was fully grown. I told you Adam was brilliant. In the beginning, he had a mind just like God's. He started talking immediately. He had an incredible vocabulary from the start. He was not God, but he was just like Him! It seemed like he could do most everything God could do. When he saw that funny thing with humps and the extra long neck, he said, 'Camel,' and that was its name."

"Incredible!" Dickens thought the camel was the goofiest animal he'd ever seen. "Boy, some of those animals are so ugly that only a mother could love them. And I suppose he knew just what to call cats when he saw 'em, right?"

"Absolutely. From the aardvark to the zebra, Adam named them all. And whatever Adam called each creature, that was the name God agreed to. And by the way, those animals didn't have a mother either; they were the mums and dads. I was just so amazed that God could think up so many different kinds of living things in the first place. I mean, who in the world could ever come up with the idea for a jellyfish? Or a rhinoceros? Or a snail? Amazing! And Adam had names for all of them. God never once interrupted or corrected him or even suggested things. It took ever so long to do this."

Shakespeare stopped talking and looked out the window. He was remembering the way his own fur had shivered when he saw this glorious parade of animals—the quacking ducks, the slithery snakes, the majestic flapping eagles—all of them coming to Adam for their names. It would surely be impossible to get every animal in the world to march so orderly in front of a human now. Of course, Shakespeare also remembered another animal parade that he had witnessed, but that was a story for a much later date.

Meanwhile, Dickens was watching his brother with semi-crossed eyes. Sometimes he just couldn't help himself; his eyes wandered close together when he was staring for a long time. What had happened to this smarty-pants brother of his all of a sudden? He was talking about jellyfish and Adam, and then he just seemed to freeze.

Dickens reached over and bonked Shakespeare right

on top of the head, much like he'd seen Mom do to the television when it was acting up. He said not a word, just bonked.

Startled out of his remembering, Shakespeare continued. "But there was more than just naming things on God's mind. In fact, God did something really strange after all the animals were named."

"What? What did he do?" Dickens had forgotten all his resolve not to let Shakespeare know how much he was interested. He was acting just like a child, asking so many questions it was nearly impossible for Shakespeare to keep his train of thought.

~ 27 ~

Of course, Shakespeare had no earthly idea how far his train of thought was going to take him that night. Everything seemed to happen all at once. Just as Shakespeare was preparing to answer Dickens' question about what happened after the naming of the animals, the telephone rang. Miss Mattie's answering machine picked up after the second ring, and her voice began to tell the caller that she wasn't at home.

And it was while this message was playing that Miss Mattie came through the door and into the sitting room. Neither of the cats had heard her steps in the corridor or her key in the door because of the distraction of the ringing phone, the blaring answering machine, and their own concentration on their story.

Oh no! Now they were really in for it! There was no way in the world that they weren't going to get discovered. Dickens had his paws on the keyboard, and the laptop was so obviously in use! Shakespeare had the chair pulled up next to the computer table, as if he were working there as well. What in the world were they to do?

It was at this point that Shakespeare did the bravest and riskiest thing he had ever done. As soon as he realized that they were going to get caught at the laptop, he leapt off the chair and made a beeline for the bedroom. At the same time, Miss Mattie walked in the sitting room and down the hall calling out, "Boys? Where are you?" As she passed the study and saw Dickens with her laptop, she heard a horrific crash from the back part of the flat!

She looked in the direction of her bedroom in horror. Forgetting what she'd seen in the study, she continued down the hall, shouting, "Shakespeare! You are going to be one homeless cat if you have just done what I think you've done!"

Miss Mattie came storming through the hallway and into her bedroom. Sure enough, there sat Shakespeare on the floor, right next to the new clock, which was then in three pieces.

He had had to work extremely hard to get this heavy clock off the shelf and onto the floor. But he had some kind of supercat resolve at that time, and in just a split second, the clock had hit the floor. The battery had fallen out the back, the plastic cover had come off the front, and the clock was dangling by the cord. It was quite a mess. It was most certainly not destroyed and could surely and easily be fixed. But Miss Mattie seemed to have reached the end of her rope.

The ensuing scolding and chasing gave Dickens enough time to save what they had just written, turn off the laptop, and hop back up on the keyboard as if he'd been sleeping there all along. Of course, by the time Miss Mattie got finished with Shakespeare, she had quite forgotten whether she had closed the laptop or not. But Dickens wasn't taking any chances. His eyes were closed, and he was snoring soundly.

Oh, and did Shakespeare ever suffer for his deed! There were so many shouts of "No! No! No! Bad boy! Bad boy!" that he lost count. He was chased and caught and had his bottom firmly smacked. He was put right to bed without his usual nighttime treat.

But he had saved the day and their story. What a close call that was! They were certainly going to have to devise a better alarm system for the next time, if there ever were a next time.

~ 28 ~

Sure enough, Miss Mattie did forgive Shakespeare. He did his best to win her over. He sat in her lap when she was trying to type on her laptop. He bumped his head into her nose and purred so loudly that he thought his throat would snap. He curled up right smack in the middle of her book. He sat by her right elbow while she sat on her bed and typed and gave both arms loads of kisses. Finally, after a day or two, Miss Mattie said "Okay, Shakespeare. I can understand that you are sorry. I forgive you, but you just have to stop this clock fetish. I can't afford to put a grandfather clock in my bedroom to wake me up in the morning!"

Dickens heard this and twitched his nose and whiskers (if he were really thinking seriously about something, this often happened). He was determined to look up the word *fetish* on the laptop dictionary next time he was using it. But a grandfather clock? What in the world was that? It was the second time he'd heard Miss Mattie mention it.

Dickens had never even known his family, of course,

so he didn't know if he had a grandfather. And he certainly didn't know that clocks could have them. He decided he'd just have to save that one and ask his know-it-all brother later. Meanwhile, he was enjoying his nap on the yellow chair. He had lots of solitude in his favorite chair while Shakespeare was on his get-Mom-to-forgive-me campaign.

When the two brothers finally got back to their story, Dickens thought he was going to burst with excitement. He had completely forgotten all about that clock and grandfather matter. This stuff was getting good!

He jumped up on the computer table and got all set up with lightening speed. Then he waited impatiently.

At last, Shakespeare finished his morning rituals and was ready to work. He got settled in his chair and began to talk. "Dickens, remember I told you that God had more than naming animals on His mind?"

Dickens was much too excited to talk, so he just nodded. Shakespeare thought this a bit odd but, nevertheless, he continued. "Well, one of the reasons that He brought all those animals to Adam was to get them named. Now understand that God already had all these animals in heaven, so He already knew their names. He could have just told them to Adam. But he wanted Adam to test how intelligent he really was, to try out that new brain, and give the names himself, you see."

Dickens did see for once. He nodded his head slowly.

"But the other reason was to see if any of them were suitable as a companion for Adam. Not like a dog or cat, but like a husband or wife, that type of companion. All the others had someone of their own kind. It was like God was waiting for Adam to say, 'Wahoo! Now, there is someone I could take home to Mama.' Only, he didn't have a mama to take anyone home to, don't you see? Adam never said anything like that or even close to it. So as soon as the parade was over, God said something really strange."

Shakespeare paused for a quick wash of his right paw, and Dickens couldn't wait. "What? What did He say?"

"Well, you might not believe this, but He actually said something was not good!"

"I knew it!" Dickens shouted with glee. "It was that camel, right? God didn't like the camels?" Dickens fairly hated the goofy-looking camel. He felt their necks entirely too long, and their walk? Completely abnormal and quite googly. "I've never liked those things. That icky humpy thing on their backs—what is that for? And I've heard they spit! They have the ugliest mouth, all slobbery, and those nasty yellow teeth and—"

Shakespeare had to stop this and stop it quickly. "No! It had nothing to do with the camels. God said it was not good that Adam had to be alone when every other thing

He had made had a husband or a wife. He wanted Adam to have someone special too, someone like him. I think God was kinda hoping that Adam would realize all by himself that there was nobody like him in that parade and maybe even ask for a helper. But it seemed that Adam was completely happy with God and just hanging out with Him that he never even thought he needed anyone else.

"Oh, yeah." Dickens was suddenly deep in thought. "That's right! He made male and female of everything else, didn't he? Adam sure couldn't be expected to marry a…a …well, yeah. So what did God do?"

"The very first thing God did was to put Adam to sleep," said Shakespeare, rather matter-of-factly.

"Say what? Put him to sleep? How? Why?" Dickens forgot all about typing. He was hopping around on the table like a little rabbit.

Shakespeare answered sadly while washing his face, "I am sorry to tell you this, Dickens. But I just do not know how. You've watched those doctor shows on TV; sometimes they use injections. Sometimes they use what humans call gas. But the effect is still the same. God was preparing Adam for surgery, and He had to put him to sleep first."

The rabbit stopped jumping and stared long and hard at his brother. "Surgery? Hello! The guy had just been

148

formed outta dirt, and you said he was perfect. What in the world did he need surgery for? This is starting to sound a little like that Frankfurter story we watched last week with Mom."

"Dickens, that was Frankenstein," Shakespeare patiently answered. This time he knew for certain that Dickens was really focusing and not just asking crazy questions.

"But this is not at all like that. Listen. God put Adam to sleep. Then He did some surgery. He took out one of Adam's ribs. I don't know how He did that either because Adam didn't have a mark on him when God finished."

Shakespeare waited for the usual outburst, but nothing came.

~ 29 ~

Dickens was too busy catching up on his typing to ask questions, so Shakespeare marched bravely on. "Now, I wasn't watching closely, so I am not at all sure how He did this next part. But one minute God was standing there with a rib in His hands, and the next minute there was a gorgeous human female standing beside him."

"Really? I don't get it. God made the female out of one of Adam's ribs? But He made Adam out of dirt?" Dickens was scratching his left ear at this turn of events. He had been typing fast and furiously, but now he stopped and turned to stare at his brother.

"That's right. Adam came from the earth because God intended for Adam to be the master of the earth. But the female came from the male. She was created from a part of him because she was made to be a perfect companion for him, absolutely equal to him and able to help Adam with anything God had for them to do. And she was just as beautiful as Adam was handsome. I guess you could say she was made to be a reflection of Adam, who was made to be a reflection of God. So even though she was not born either, she was different. The female was created as a companion for the man, not a companion for God. Adam was the one created as a companion for God."

Shakespeare felt as if he were talking in circles, but he was trying very hard to explain this difficult concept to Dickens. He was trying to explain the created-in-his-image part, which was hard enough the first time but nearly impossible the second time around. It was almost—almost, but not quite—confusing him as well.

He decided to have a quick scratch under his collar. The bell jingled like an ice cream truck while he scratched. Then, seeing the position of Dickens' whiskers, he decided to have one more go.

"Okay, remember the Rockwell painting? I told you that God created Adam as if he had been looking in a mirror, right?"

This was something, finally, that seemed clear to Dickens, so he nodded his head—not quite enough to make his bell jingle—but he nodded nonetheless.

Shakespeare plodded on. "Well, I guess you could say that with the female, God was not looking in the mirror. He was looking at Adam."

Shakespeare relaxed and sat down, thinking that at last he had done it. Even though he was an eyewitness to all this creation, Shakespeare had to admit that he had missed quite a few things. He just didn't see God put the breath in the man, and he wasn't quite sure how he had put Adam to sleep. And the pattern for the female—how did he miss that? Honestly, it would be good for a fellow to pay more attention.

Dickens wrinkled his eye whiskers and said, "But, um, Shakes? Adam was a male. That is a boy/man/guy, right? How could God be looking at Adam, who was made in his image, and come up with a female? That is a girl/woman, right?"

Before Shakespeare tried to answer this one, he took a deep breath and counted to ten slowly. "Well, ole boy, I guess you could say that God got in touch with His feminine side."

Shakespeare surprised even himself with that humorous answer. "Since everything God created had come out of his mind, you could say that both male and female exist in him. That's not to say that he is a she but that all living beings have their origins in him, both male and female. So, when He made Adam, He made him with male and female characteristics. And when He put him to sleep, it was as if God just took all the female parts out of him and used them to create the woman. Is this making any sense?"

Shakespeare was sitting up tall at this point and looking out the window, concentrating really hard. So many things to say and such a hard concept to get across. He just had to make Dickens understand this, both for Dickens's sake and for the sake of their story.

"I think so," Dickens said, but he was more puzzled than sure. "And that's the part that scares me."

He looked over at Shakespeare then looked quickly back again. "Say, Shakes, you know something? You look sorta like a black and white polka dot bowling pin from the back." Dickens knew about bowling because he liked to watch it on the television with his mom.

Shakespeare very wisely chose to ignore this observation and continued with his story. He turned from looking out the window at the beautiful, cloudless sky and continued. "Well, think about it, Dickens, ole boy. In humans, at least, there's very little difference between the males and females. One is curvier than the other, and some things stick out on one and don't on the other, or as mom always says, 'one has indoor plumbing and one has outdoor plumbing.' But males and females have a lot of similarities."

Shakespeare cautioned himself to keep this simple, or he was going to be accused of teaching a biology lesson as well as chemistry! Dickens, as usual, provided just the distraction needed to keep things from becoming too serious. "And the belly button? Did she have one?"

This time Shakespeare was almost grateful for the

silly question. It gave him a chance to catch his breath. He answered patiently, "No, Dickens. Humans have belly buttons because of the scar that forms when the cord is cut. This cord is what connects the baby to the mother until it is born and starts to live outside her body. It's like a lifeline from the mother to the baby. Adam and the female did not have a mother, a cord, or a scar."

"I'll bet Adam was totally blown away when he woke up, right?" Dickens asked his brother. He sat back on his haunches, curled his you-know-what around his body, and smiled at the thought. He had already forgotten about that belly button. He was thinking how swell it would be if God were to bring him a beautiful wife!

"Absolutely right. When Adam woke up, God brought that female to him to see what Adam would name her. He was, as you say, completely blown away. He had watched the animal parade and named all the animals. But this one was completely different. Everything else that had been brought to him had been in pairs. But this one was alone. There weren't any mirrors, so he really didn't realize that she looked like him, but he just knew that she was different from all the other animals."

Dickens interrupted. "Yeah, I'll say she was different! But when did she get her name?"

Shakespeare said, "Well, God told him how he had made this female, and then Adam named her *woman* because she came from his bones and flesh. Woman was her animal name, like our animal name is cat. Her human name was Eve. Now Adam was not alone anymore. He had a companion just like all the other animals. They were wonderful together, but they looked a bit odd to me."

Shakespeare's eyes were narrowed as he remembered his first look at this human couple. He so wanted to tell Dickens about his epiphany: woman was like "womb man." She was just like the man in so many areas, but she had the womb from which other humans would be born. What an idea! But even in the thinking of it, Shakespeare knew he couldn't brave the troubled waters of Dickens' brain to try and sort this one out. He merely shook his head.

Dickens stopped typing and looked at his brother expectantly. He noticed that head shake and said, "Odd? Why?"

Shakespeare turned his head really far to one side. He really hadn't intended to get into this area, but he had a quick wash of his large white foot and said, "Well, Dickens, all the animals had fur or hair. The birds had feathers, and the fish had scales or something. But these two humans were just wearing light brown skin. No fur, no feathers, no scales, nothing."

"Nothing? You mean they weren't wearing any

clothes?" Dickens' eyes were really wide! He had never seen a human without any clothes on. Oh, there were plenty of television shows, but the humans always had on diapers or neckties or something. He couldn't imagine this sight.

"Nope! They weren't. Babies don't wear any clothes when they're born, you know!"

Dickens couldn't quite take this in. "Yeah, but people put clothes on 'em right away, don't they? I thought only really old or really poor or really peculiar humans went around without any clothes. What's up with this?"

"Well, think about it, Dickens," began Shakespeare with a twinkle in his eye. "Where would they buy clothes? There was absolutely nothing on the earth except animals, fish, birds, and Adam and Eve. They didn't need clothes to express their personalities or to keep warm. They didn't need clothes for work, to go to the theatre, to play sports. God had prepared everything so perfectly for them. Adam didn't have to do a thing except breathe and enjoy the world around him. He and Eve were sort of wearing glory suits, clothed in some of that fantastically bright glory of God. If you had been there you would have noticed how shiny and bright they were. Remember I told you that wherever God is, there is this incredible light? Well, the name for that light is glory; it's like God is reflecting Himself."

At the look on Dickens' face, Shakespeare quickly decided not to continue that line of the story. Instead, he simply said, "They didn't need anything. It was like He was their clothing. Yes. That's it. They were made in God's image, so—"

When he realized what Shakespeare was saying (or what he thought he was saying), Dickens jumped into this with all four feet. "God was naked too?"

Uh oh. This was a serious mistake! Shakespeare completely lost the plot at this point. "No! God was not naked! God is a Spirit! When you look at Him, it seems as though He wears a white robe, a long white robe, so white that it looks like millions of stars, like dozens of bottles of Clorox have washed it, like blazing fire, like thousands of cars with their lights on, like a gazillion fireflies, like—"

"Okay, Shakes. I got it. Calm down now. Breathe. Breathe. That's it." Dickens realized that Shakespeare was dangerously close to a total snap! He seemed to realize that if he didn't keep Shakespeare on the right track, he (Dickens) would never get the rest of the story.

"And then . . ." Shakespeare began again when he had finished calming down. There was a long pause, a really long pause. So long that Dickens stopped typing and looked hard at Shakespeare. "And then what?"

~ 30 ~

Shakespeare was trying to decide how much of this next part to tell Dickens at this time and how much to save for the next time. He was seriously hoping that before there was a next time, he could find someone else to do his typing for him! There had been one point where he thought Dickens was really close to understanding, but after this clothing episode, all his doubts had returned.

"Well, this gets really complicated, and our story is getting much too long. I think I want to save some for another story, book, file, or whatever it is we're writing here."

Shakespeare thought that Dickens would be happy to hear that he was ready for a short vacation. Once again, Shakespeare had misjudged his brother. For Dickens, in spite of his earlier resolve, was really getting into this story.

"No way, Jose! You stop now and that would be like when Mom and her friends were watching that Albert Hillchock movie and it got right to the last five minutes and the tape broke. Remember how they howled?"

Dickens was looking at Shakespeare with a frighteningly intelligent look. That meant he was sitting up straight, legs properly together, feet and toes straight, you-know-what curled majestically around his rump, eyes clear and looking straight ahead.

It didn't fool Shakespeare, however. "Alfred Hitchcock, Dickens. Really!"

The correction didn't faze him a bit. Dickens was seriously intent on this topic. "C'mon, Shakes. Tell me!"

Shakespeare thought for a moment while he had a quick face wash. He slowly licked first one paw pad and then the other, rubbed each foot over his eyes, ears, and nose. He worked furiously on his eyes because they always had crusties in the corners. Mom hated those crusties.

When the wash was completed, he continued. "Well, then, let me just say this much. First of all, God made Adam. He put him in a gorgeous green garden. God took Adam right to the middle of the garden and showed him two special trees. The tree in the very center was one God called the Tree of Knowledge, and the other tree was called the Tree of Life. He told Adam that he could have fruit from any tree in the garden but one—the Tree of Knowledge. That one he was most certainly not supposed to eat from."

Dickens interrupted Shakespeare as he was talking.

He completely stopped typing and looked at his brother. Nothing was itching for once. "Huh? Wait a minute. All the plants, trees, flowers, and grass He had created, and He gave only two of them names? I don't get it." Dickens right cheek was pulled up as he scrunched up his eye; he did this when thinking, but it was such a goofy look that it always made Shakespeare laugh.

"Neither did I at the time," admitted Shakespeare as he surveyed his right paw, trying hard not to laugh. "But remember I told you that everything God does has a reason. He told Adam that he could have anything in the garden he wanted but not any fruit from the tree in the middle. It was a sort of test."

Dickens looked up from the laptop. "A test? Brand new, just created—and already a test?"

"Yes and after God made Eve, He told them the same thing He had told all the other living things: to get busy and start having babies. He wanted the whole earth full of the things He'd created, but He wanted each individual creature to have a part in the population growth." He stopped to see how this information was being received. So far so good. "God intended for Adam to explain the rules of the game to Eve and to tell her about which trees were off limits. Actually there was only one—the Tree of Knowledge."

"Wow," said Dickens. "Why? Seems to me that

knowledge would be something that Eve would need to have a lot of. After all, she was the second one in."

Dickens seemed to be thinking a bit about his own arrival in the Davis family and how he always felt he just couldn't measure up to his older brother in the intelligence or experience area. He was thinking himself into quite a scowl.

At this point, Shakespeare was busily washing between his toes. "I'll explain it all to you later, little one. Right now, I'm a bit tired. Let's just imagine how tired God was after this long and adventure-filled day. He looked around at every living creature he had made, at his magnificent man and woman, and he pronounced it all very good! And that, dear brother, was the end of day six!"

~ 31 ~

"Uh, Shakes?" Dickens asked quickly. "Just exactly how many days are there in this story? We might need to think about how we're going to store all this information on the laptop." Just exactly how they were going to do this was a knotty little problem that Dickens was chewing on during his off-duty hours. The file was growing to an alarming size, and he feared it might prove impossible to hide.

"Well, Dickens. I was just about to tell you this. There's only one more day. And absolutely nothing happened on this day."

I'm not quite sure about this, but I think Shakespeare might have been smiling! He was certainly happy about finishing his foot washing.

"No way! How do you explain that?"

"Easy. You know how Mom gets some days of vacation from her job every year? Every person who works gets some kind of holiday. This is exactly what God had—a rest day. He did nothing on this day."

"So," began Dickens, "God needed a rest?"

Shakespeare stopped work on his toes and looked up at his brother. "No, He certainly did not need a rest. He wasn't tired. He just created a day for all of His creation to stop what they were doing and enjoy their lives. He intended this day to be a day of thinking about him and all He'd done for the earth and its inhabitants. His work of creation was finished; there was nothing left to do. So He stopped and we all went home. He left His earth, His people, His animals, and His plants, and just went home. He intended to come back every day to check on Adam and Eve and visit with them. But for that day and that job, He was done. He wanted the man and woman He'd made to do the same—just relax and enjoy."

Shakespeare stopped to smooth an out-of-place hair on his you-know-what.

Dickens was typing, but he still asked, "So there were just seven days in this deal, right?"

"Right," said Shakespeare. "This is how people got the concept of a seven-day week. We didn't have clocks then, so I'm just not sure how long each one of those days was. I just know that God started counting his days with evening and ended with evening, but how many hours were in it, I do not know."

Dickens fingers were flying, but this stopped him midword! "The day started with evening and ended with evening? Don't you have that a bit messed up?"

Shakespeare looked so comical trying to lick the fur down on his back. He was so fat that this task always made him flip over on his side. Dickens loved to watch this and always thought long and hard about telling his brother he might consider whatever new diet was all the rage at that moment. (Of course, he never actually spoke these thoughts out loud, but it was quite fun to imagine doing so.)

The seasoned storyteller quickly righted himself and sat up straight. "No, as odd as it seems, I do not have it wrong way round. God does things differently and thinks differently than His creation. He considers the beginning of the day to be just before sunset. In Mom's Bible, these stories are written, 'And the evening and the morning were the first day'. . . second day . . . third day . . . and so forth. Odd, eh?"

Dickens thought it much more than odd. In fact, it was just crazy. How could a day start when people were asleep? That was a curious thing, for sure. What Dickens did not know (and his brother was much too exhausted to try to explain) is that technically, a day begins a second after midnight, not when the sun comes up the following morning. It seemed much more economical to say that when the sun left, that was the end of the day and when it came back, that was the start of the next. Now how that all fit together with "the evening and the morning were the first day" was quite a puzzle, even to Shakespeare.

However the day is measured, Shakespeare wanted to get this chapter closed and get on with dinner and a nice sleep. "Regardless of when the day started or began, for many centuries humans have had one day of rest in their weeks. For most people, that day is a Sunday. Surely, I find it a bit strange that some humans spend their day of rest either working or going to meetings all day. But what God intended for His people to do on this day was to spend it remembering how great He is, how much He loves them, how much He did for them, and to share that love with their families and friends. But somewhere, things got a bit muddled, didn't they?"

He was trying to wash behind his neck, a very difficult place to reach. Soon Shakespeare's eyes began to get heavy. Telling this story had taken a lot out of him, both the remembering and the difficulties with his assistant. Now he was ready for his well-earned day of rest. He had much more to tell but he wanted to give it to Dickens in smaller increments. After all, they'd been working on the seven days for months and just got to the end. Yes, he definitely deserved a long nap.

On the other side of the room, Dickens just couldn't believe it. They were finished. All the typing, all the ear scratching, all the arguing and bickering—now it was over. He couldn't believe it was true, but he actually felt sad. As they walked to the food bowls, Dickens said softly.

"Shakes, can I ask you just one teensy weensy little question?"

Yawning one of his famous and quite ferocious yawns, Shakespeare simply said, "Hmm?"

Dickens then proceeded to ask about something he'd seen on the television, something the TV people called "The Big Bang." Over his most fervent doubts and surely against his better judgment, while munching on their dry food bits, Shakespeare attempted to answer this question even though extremely sleepy.

"Oh, yes, little one, there was *quite* a bang. When God spoke, 'BE . . . ,' everything in creation vibrated."

Finished with his snack, Shakespeare started towards the sitting room with Dickens close behind. As he hopped up onto their favorite yellow chair and began to settle himself into nap position, Shakespeare continued, "My ears felt as though some gigantic fire truck had just exploded next to my head. It was a bang all right. Now go to sleep!"

And he also said something that made Dickens quite happy. Shakespeare sleepily told Dickens, "No, my sweet baby brother, this is most certainly not the end. So much more to come—wars, mysteries, love stories, dramas, miracles—so much more."

Dickens, not so sure about the love stories, quickly said "Miracles? What's that?"

Shakespeare answered sleepily, "I need sleep, Dickens. You'll have to wait for the proper time to start the next episode. You can practice exercising your faith, how about that? But just know, it is not the end. In fact, it is only the beginning."

And so it was time for the two brothers to have a nice long rest. Curled up together in their favorite chair, snug as always, two brothers began to dream, all upsets between them quickly forgotten.

ABOUT THE AUTHOR

M E WELDON holds degrees in European History/Humanities and TESL from Oral Roberts University in Tulsa, Oklahoma, as well as coursework for a PhD in Victorian Lit from the University of Tulsa. She is a gifted teacher of English, all things musical and has focused on children's ministries all her adult life. When not traveling and teaching overseas, she can be found at home with her cats Shakespeare, Dickens and Lady Jane (Janey) Austen in Fort Worth, Texas.

The author may be contacted through her website at www.meweldon.com.